CONTENTS

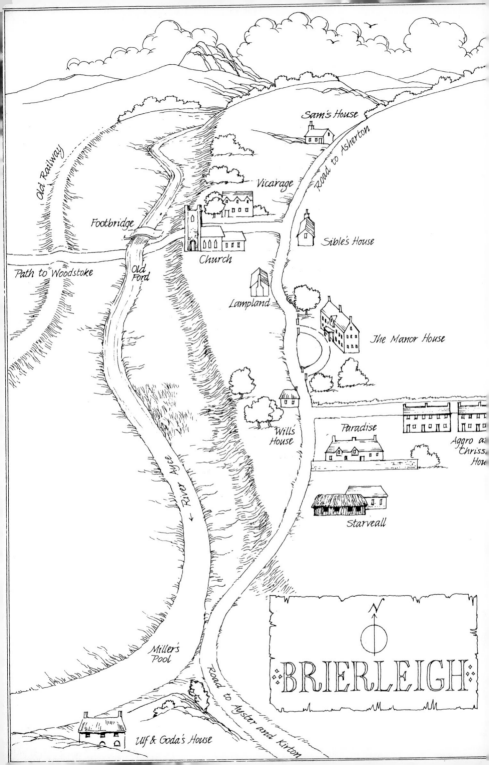

Nobody has heard of Brierleigh. It isn't a big, important or famous village – just three or four dozen houses (old and new, thatched and tiled), strung along a country lane by a river. It has a church, a school, a shop and a village hall. But people have lived in Brierleigh for over a thousand years and, during all that time, stories have been happening there. This book tells you some of the stories.

Chapter 1

WHITE BIRD FLYING

A rider galloped his horse, its feet thundering on the hard, frozen ground. Behind him, holding on to his waist, was a boy. Above their heads the sky loomed dreary grey – the sort of sky which says that snow is coming. The rider was a well-built man, with fair hair, but the boy was black-haired, with a dark tinge to his skin. They were not related.

Wade, the man, lived in Brierleigh and had a small farm there. For a long time he had been looking for a boy to work for him, but there were many farmers in the world and no one wanted to send his son to Wade. Then, just before Christmas, he had heard about a boy in a village fifteen miles away, whose stepfather was willing to sell him as a servant. Wade had to pay a number of silver coins before the man agreed that he could take the boy and own him for ten years. Today, Wade had ridden over to fetch him. It was the 5th of January.

Wade turned the horse's head to the right and slackened the speed. They left the road and entered a wide and level stretch of land, dotted with bramble bushes and clumps of reeds. It was marshy ground. Had it not been frozen, the ground would have been difficult to cross because there was no clear path. Ahead of them, a low ridge could be seen with what turned out, as they got nearer, to be a river in front of it. The ridge was brown with bracken and the only building on it was a small, oblong tower, coloured dingy white. Wade turned his head and shouted to the boy, "That's the tower! We shall be home soon."

To the boy, peering from behind the rider's back, the view

ahead looked as dull and cheerless as the place he had left. But to Wade, the tower was always a stirring sight. He could see it from his house in the village and he had first climbed to its top with the help of his father when he was only three or four. It guarded the spot where the winding track through the marshes reached the river and crossed the water by a shallow ford. People said that the Romans had built the tower to watch the river and to get warning of enemies approaching the great city of Ayster, half a dozen miles away. The Romans had gone home long ago and a Saxon lord had built a church there with mud walls, meaning to use the tower to hang a bell in. The bell was never hung, or if it was it had been stolen, and now the church had fallen into ruin. Yet the tower still remained. It was so well built that it stayed as it was, even though no one bothered to repair it.

It was because of the tower that Wade was a farmer. Years and years ago, a king had come riding that way with an army. They had trouble finding the ford and the king saw the value of the old tower as a landmark. He ordered the walls to be whitewashed to show up in the daytime and a lantern to shine for those who travelled at night. Wade's great- or great-great-grandfather had been chosen to light the lantern and his family had done it ever since. In return, they were allowed to farm a few fields in the village and their house and land came to be known as Lampland.

While Wade had ridden off to fetch his new boy servant, Aelf his daughter had been making the candles. This was a good task for a winter day because she could work by the fire. The fire was in the centre of the house and sent its smoke up through a hole in the roof. First, she filled an old iron pot with lumps of fat and hung it on the fire to melt the fat. Then she got ready a bundle of reeds, making sure they were strong, dry and not broken. Next, she brought out the candle mould. This was made of the two halves of a log, scooped out and tied together so that it formed a hollow cylinder. She also had a bucket of cold water.

She poured the melted fat out of the pot into the upright mould. Holding the mould in a glove because the wood grew hot, she took a reed, dipped it into the fat, took it out and put it into the water. The fat dried into a white waxy covering. She put the reed back into the mould and added another layer of wax, cooled it, and went on thickening the wax in the same way. A few dips were enough to make a rushlight for burning in the hall, or lighting yourself to bed. But she also needed to make candles for the lantern in the tower. It took a great many dippings and another filling of the mould to make a candle thick enough to burn through a long winter night.

She had been working for some time and the daylight was beginning to fade, when she heard a fumbling at the latch of the door. She looked up, expecting her father to open the door, but the door remained shut. The fumbling went on, so she got up and opened the door. There was a boy outside, a strange boy. He looked scared. "Is this Wade's house?" he said.

"Yes," she answered. "What do you want?"

"Your father sent me," the boy said. "He was bringing me here. He's hurt." She gasped. "The horse slipped as we were crossing the ford. It fell on his leg."

Aelf went pale. "We must go to him," she said. "I'll get my cloak." She looked at him more closely. "You're wet. Are you hurt too?"

"No," said the boy. "I'm not hurt. And he – he's coming. He sent me to another house to get help. Two people are bringing him here. He said to get his bed ready and hot water."

"What's your name?" she said.

"Eddi," he replied.

"Mine is Aelf," she said. She held out a hand and he took it, awkwardly. "Eddi, you had better stand by the fire and get dry." She went over to the fire, filled a large pot with water from a bucket and put it on to heat. Then she took a smooth stone from beside the fire where it had been heating, wrapped it in a cloth and carried it into the sleeping room next to the hall. She took off the covers of her father's bed, which was built into the wall like a bunk and put in the stone to warm the bed. There was a noise at the door. Eddi opened it. Two men came in, carrying a hurdle. Aelf's father was lying on it. They put him down near the fire. Hilda, the old woman who lived next door and looked after them, hovered behind. There was a babble of voices.

"Lay him down carefully – easy does it."

"Is someone seeing to the horse?"

"Yes. It's not badly hurt, I think, just grazed on the side."

"Father! How are you?"

"Badly bruised in the leg, girl. The horse fell on me. And I knocked my head."

"Let me wash his wounds." This from Hilda. "Then we'll put him into a warm bed. Aelf, get a stone from the fire."

"I've done it already, Hilda."

Half an hour later, Wade's cloak and leggings had been taken off and his wounds washed. He had been given a restoring drink of hot ale and put into bed. Acca the woodcutter, who

knew about plants and medicines, had looked at the wounds
and said that the knock on the head would make Wade dizzy for
a day or two. The bruised leg would probably turn black. But
nothing had been broken, and a few days rest in bed would cure
everything.

"You'll just have to lie here and be quiet," said Acca. "That
leg'll be stiff and sore by tomorrow, though."

"I can do that," said Wade weakly. "But I can't light the
lantern in the tower. That's what worries me."

Acca wondered, as he often did, why Wade took so much
trouble with the tower. "It will do without a light for a few days,"
he said. "There aren't many travellers about in midwinter. Give
yourself a rest."

Aelf looked surprised. Her father – who had lain patiently
while his wounds were dealt with – stirred restlessly. "It must be
lit. It's our duty. I've done it for fifteen years and my father and
grandfather before me. It's never been missed."

"Well, now's the time to miss it," said Hilda. "Who sees that
old lamp anyway? Many's a time I've watched you go off to light
it in the evening and thought why doesn't he stay by the fire?"

Wade spoke loudly; a feverish colour was already appearing
on his face. "It has to be done. Remember the old king, Ecgbert!
He came in anger with his men against the Cornish, seventy
years ago. You've heard that story. There were a dozen towers
between here and Winchester which should have had lights in,
and he found the lights were out. He called for the lightkeepers
and had them flogged until they cried for mercy. He came into
our village in the evening and saw our lamp lit. He stopped his
horse by the tower and called for my grandfather. 'You have
done your duty well,' he said, 'but see that you do it still!' He

drew his sword half out of its sheath and put it back again. Then he rode on. No thanks or reward did he give, only the promise that if ever the light went out, it would be the worse for the lightkeeper."

There was a silence. Nobody liked to say anything. Acca shrugged his shoulders and said, "Well, I'll light the lantern for you tonight, friend Wade, if that will help you sleep."

"No!" said Wade. "I thank you for the offer, Acca, and for all your help, but the duty is laid on our house and Aelf must do it if I can't. She can take the boy with her for company – and they had better go now, for night is coming on."

The neighbours said goodbye and moved out of the house, except for Hilda who stayed behind to prepare food, muttering to herself. Wade spoke again to Aelf. "Go up and light the lamp," he said. "And then come back into the warm. Eddi, you go with her and do what she tells you."

Aelf took a lantern from the wall, lit the candle inside with a bit of wood from the fire and shut the lantern window. She put on her cloak and smiled at the boy. He followed her outside; it was cold and the daylight was fading. Eddi felt shy and awkward; what ought he to say? But Aelf started talking immediately. She said, "I'm sorry this happened. You should have had a better homecoming. Tomorrow, we will get things settled and find you somewhere good to sleep. At least you won't be hungry tonight. Hilda seems cross sometimes, but she cooks well."

He said, "That's all right."

"How big is your family?" she asked.

"Quite big," he said. "I've got six brothers and sisters but they're not really mine – I'm their stepbrother."

"I wish I had brothers and sisters," she said, "or stepbrothers.

There's only me and my father." He said nothing.

By this time they had turned into a lane, passed the ruined church and reached the tower itself. It loomed up bulkily above them. There was a door at the bottom. Aelf pushed this open and led the way inside. There was no window and it was hard to see anything until their eyes got used to the darkness. Presently, Eddi could make out a ladder, leading to a hole in the wooden floor above. Aelf started to climb the ladder, holding her lantern in one hand and gripping the rungs with the other. Eddi followed. They emerged on to a wooden floor, with a dim light coming in from a tiny window. A second ladder led to a similar hole. They climbed that too, into the top storey of the tower. Here, the roof was higher, held up by sloping rafters with thatch on top. In each of the four walls was a round-arched window with glass in it, about three feet from the floor. A large lantern hung from the rafters, placed so that it would shine in all directions, like the light of a lighthouse.

A rough, wooden stepladder stood under the lantern. Aelf lit a spill from her own candle, climbed the stepladder, opened the big lantern and lit it too. "There," she said, "that will burn all night – there is plenty of candle."

"Do people really need it to cross the ford?" asked Eddi.

"Oh yes, sometimes. Some travellers get lost in the dark and make their way towards the light, especially on stormy nights in winter. They often ask for shelter when they get here."

They were about to walk back to the hole in the floor when Aelf stopped suddenly. "What's that?" she said, sharply.

There was a rustling noise. It seemed to come from close by. Then there was silence.

"Was it a rat?" asked Eddi.

"There aren't rats this high up." They turned to go. The rustling came again. Eddi hesitated. "I can see something," he said. "It's over there."

Aelf waved the lantern. Something white fluttered in one of the windows. They both winced, wondering what it was. A huge moth?

"It's a bird," said Aelf. They went over to it cautiously. It was white, like a dove, its feathers soft and gleaming in the lamplight. It looked at them, but did not try to fly.

"It must have got in through a hole," she said. "We must catch it and take it outside, or else it will die." She put out her hand and stroked it. It showed no sign of fear. She picked it up. "It seems to be tame," she said. Then – "Look!" she pointed to its legs. One had a label on it, tied with string. "Is it a message?"

She held the bird, while Eddi examined the label. "It's got letters on it," he said. "Runes. I don't know what they mean."

"I learnt them from Father," she said. "You hold the bird and I'll look." They changed places. She held the label in her fingers and peered at it. There were two words.

"What does it say?" asked Eddi.

"It means, 'The king is coming'," she replied.

"What king?"

"The king. Our king. Like the other ones came. This must be a messenger bird. It can't have been here long, or else the king would have come already. It must have flown in here for shelter; it was windy last night."

"When will the king come?" asked Eddi.

"Tonight?" she said. "Tomorrow morning? Some time soon. It's a good thing Father didn't listen to the woodcutter. The lantern may be needed to guide the king this very night."

"What shall we do?"

"Let's take the bird downstairs and let it go. It may have to fly further on. Then we'll go back and tell Father," said Aelf. Very carefully, one carrying the bird and the other the lantern, they went downstairs. They pushed open the tower door and saw it was dark outside. There was something in the air: a few snowflakes were coming down. They let the bird go and it spread its wings strongly, with no sign of weakness. It showed pure white for a moment in the light of the lantern, then it flew eastwards. As it flew, Eddi was reminded of something. What was it? He stared after the bird as it disappeared into the night.

They started to return towards Wade's house. Eddi looked up at the tower. He said timidly, "Why can't you see the light through the window?"

"You can," said Aelf. "It's up there." She looked; the window was dark. "I don't understand," she said. "Surely the light isn't out? I'd better go back and look."

She ran back to the tower, with Eddi following. They climbed the stairs. The topmost storey was quite dark. The lantern had gone out.

"Bother!" she said. She lit another spill from her lantern, climbed up and relit the large lantern. She examined it carefully. "It doesn't seem to be wet," she said. "Well, it's all right now." They made their way down again and out into the open. They looked up. The window was bright.

They continued their way home, with the snowflakes falling around them. Further on, Eddi again felt an impulse to turn back. He clutched at Aelf's arm. "Look at the window!"

The light in the window was flickering bright and dim, as if the candle in the lantern was guttering. As they watched, it flashed once and went out.

"It must be something to do with the candle," said Aelf. "We'll get another and come back and light it." She spoke pleasantly, but Eddi felt that she was worried. Something was the matter. Why wouldn't the light stay lit?

When they got back to the house, Hilda was there, getting the supper: bowls of thick soup. Their father had eaten his and gone to sleep. "Have your supper now," said Hilda. "Then you can sit by the fire and get warm."

"We'd like our supper," said Aelf, "but we have got to go back to the tower. The light has gone out."

Hilda was horrified. "Going out on a freezing night like this, up that old haunted tower! You'll catch your deaths of cold! I don't know what your father is about, filling your head with ideas about that lantern. All the years he's lit it and what good has it brought him? He's no richer than ever he was. What good did it do him when he went out against the Danes and got his wound, or when your mother died? He's been a slave to that lamp and I've no patience with it."

She poured the soup out, with a sour face. Aelf sat down at the table. Eddi remained standing. "Come and eat," said Aelf. "It's for you too." He sat down warily. The soup was good and had all sorts of vegetables in it. There were pieces of crusty wholemeal bread as well.

After supper, Hilda went home to her own house. Aelf got up. "Now," she said, "we must go back. We'll take a new candle." She took one of the store she had made that afternoon, put on her cloak, picked up the lantern and they left.

Again, they went along the frozen road. The snow was falling thicker now, making a white covering on the ground. They pushed open the tower door and went up the ladders. The darkness sprang away at the sight of their lantern, but something struck Eddi as odd. Of course it was cold, you would expect that. But an icy draught seemed to play round his head for a moment and then disappear. It must be coming in through a hole.

Aelf climbed the stepladder, opened the tower lantern and took out the candle. She examined it. "It's odd," she said. "It is quite dry and the wick is sound. Anyway, we'll try the other one." She put in the new candle, lit it and shut the lantern door.

"Let's watch it for a bit," said Eddi, "and see what happens."

They stood at the side of the room in silence. Again, Eddi felt a cold draught go by his neck. A few seconds later, the candle flame began to flicker violently. Aelf rushed to the lantern. Immediately, the flame steadied and brightened.

"There's nothing else for it," said Aelf. "We shall have to watch the lantern all night." She paused for a moment. "Something is wrong with it." Once more, Eddi had the feeling that she was trying not to mention something. She spoke again. "Father said this has happened before. You have to watch it all night, then."

"It will be very cold," said Eddi.

"We'll light a fire. Father has done that sometimes. He makes it on the ledge beneath that window." She pointed to a small pile of ashes and charred sticks. "If you go down to the lane, you can get some sticks and bring them up. Then, during the night, we'll take turns. One of us ought to stay with Father."

Eddi went down to look for fuel while Aelf watched the lantern. There was a hedge opposite the tower with an ash tree in it – a good place to look for sticks. He collected several armfuls; then he climbed up and down the ladders, taking a load at a time.

When he came up with the last sticks, Aelf had lit a fire from her lantern and it was crackling on the stone window ledge. The fire made the room more cheerful. Aelf said, "Would you like me to watch first, or you? We can divide the night into two."

Eddi said, "I am not tired yet. I don't mind staying, if you want to go home first."

"All right," she said. "I'll come back soon after midnight. I'll sit up in a chair and then if I go to sleep, I shan't sleep for long."

She went down, taking her lantern with her. He heard her clatter down the ladders and out of the door. It became very quiet. He could hear only the sound of the fire crackling the sticks. Occasionally, there was a hiss as it reached one that was wet with frost or snow.

He sat for some time, warming himself at the fire and watching the dancing shadows on the wall. He felt tired after the long, disturbing day.

Then he suddenly jerked awake. The fire had burnt down to embers. Something had woken him up. He felt it again, the draught on his neck, like the breath of a cold creature. The light in the lantern flickered and danced. Then to his horror, it went out. The room was suddenly dark, except for the red embers where the fire had been. He had a moment of panic. He must put on more twigs before the embers went out. He reached and could not find them. He bent over and again he felt the cold breath on his neck. He scrabbled, found the twigs and put several on the embers. He felt threatened by something he could not see. He stood with his back to the embers and once more the cold draught played around him. Just when he thought he could not bear the darkness any longer, a stick caught fire and light flared up. There was a sound like a sigh –

not a sigh of contentment or rest, but a sigh of despair. He took a burning stick in his hand, climbed the stepladder and relit the lantern. Then he put some more sticks on the fire.

It was a little later that the sounds began. At first, it was like someone talking, a very long way away. Muffled bits of whispering. He wondered if Aelf was coming back with a neighbour. He went to the hole in the floor and listened, but no one was climbing up. The whispering started again. Could it be a leaf blowing inside? The sound turned to a kind of hushed voice. It seemed as if unseen lips were speaking a message into his ear. The hair on his neck tingled. What could this be? The wind, perhaps, would make a noise in the tower. But then he remembered that the night was still; there had not been a breath of wind when they came to the tower. So it could not be wind that made this sobbing sound, like a moan, seeming to come from outside the windows.

Again, he felt panic. The lantern flickered and guttered. He got ready another lighted stick. As before, this seemed to steady the flame in the lantern. He had a curious thought. "The flame and I are together. We are both for the light, against the dark. We are for the king, against the enemy." This was comforting. He stood up, holding his lighted twig, and drew a bright line in the air. Then he drew another across it. The moan from outside changed from menace to fear and pain. It faded; in fact it seemed to pass into the distance, flying away to some dim wood or cave.

Then there were footsteps. Someone was coming up the ladders. Was it Aelf? He caught the glimmer of a lantern. Her head came through the hole and he shook himself awake. "It's very cold here," she said. "I've brought you some hot ale to warm you up." She gave him a leather tankard, warm to the touch. He drank the hot liquid gratefully, feeling it flow through his body, driving out the cold.

After a while, she said hesitantly, "I am worried about leaving Father. He is feverish, his sleep is broken and he is not clear where he is."

He looked at her. He knew what he had to say. "I don't mind staying here," he said.

She gave him a grateful look. "I shall stay awake too and I'll be thinking of you. If he wakes up and asks, I'll be able to say that you're keeping the light. But you need more firewood. I'll help you get some. You'll freeze if you don't keep the fire going."

"I'll come down with you," he said. He followed her down and outside. There was enough snow now to show where the bushes were and they were able to gather some more piles of sticks and carry them into the tower. "You go home now," he said. "I can manage."

"Thank you," she said. She waved to him and walked away through the snow.

He went back into the tower and started taking up the sticks. When he came down for the last time he saw that the door was still open, so he closed it, hoping it might keep him warmer. The door was difficult to shut and he had to tug it sharply before it jammed itself into place. He climbed the ladders again, put more sticks on the fire and sat down beside it. The tower was absolutely silent. The flame in the lantern rose up still and clear. Whatever ghosts had been there, threatening the light, they had gone.

He thought again about the day. When he had come here on

the horse, he had expected another place of hard work and beatings, like home. But it had not been like that. The man, when the horse had thrown them, had not cursed; he had lain there calmly saying what to do. The girl had welcomed him, invited him to the table. It all reminded him of something a long time ago. What was it? The white bird had reminded him too.

Then a picture came into his memory. It was a winter's day, in the open air. He was a tiny child riding on his father's shoulder, walking along a road. Snowflakes were coming down and hitting him on the nose. And his father sang him a song – how did it go? "White bird flying … " Yes, he remembered it exactly, after all those years. He said it over to himself again:

> "White bird flying by,
> Coming down from the sky,
> Fir, furrow, house, hall,
> White bird covers all."

What did it mean? It must be a riddle. The white bird is the snow which covers everything. But how beautiful it was, the picture it gave: dark green trees and snug thatched houses under the clean white snow. He felt tears come into his eyes – at something beautiful that he had lost. Would he find it again in this new place?

Time went on. The night seemed endless. The cold was intense. He cowered over the fire, rubbing his hands. The flames scorched his skin, but seemed incapable of warming his body. After a bit, he gave up and sat on the floor under the window ledge. The excitement he had felt died away. He had never known such silence: it seemed as though the whole world had stopped, beyond the little crackles coming out of his fire. It was as if the silence had melted away the walls of the tower and he could hear along the whole of time and space, for miles and miles and hundreds and hundreds of years. They stretched away, vast and empty, like the spaces in the sky between the stars.

Only, the spaces were not quite empty. There was something out there, something coming towards him from a great distance away. It had a long way to come, but it was getting closer. What was it? Not a spirit from the past – some Roman ghost – for they were weak and they had done their worst with their whispering and moaning, and he had driven them away with the flame. No, this was a stronger spirit, a living spirit, and it did not come from the past, but along the roads and through the marshes – the very journey he had made today. It was following him, gliding over the ground, slipping across the ford and soon it would climb the ladders. It was the spirit of his stepfather, with the belt in his hand – like last night and many nights before – coming back drunk from the inn and looking for him.

He felt himself growing weak and faint. The silent thing was coming up the ladders, pushing its shoulders through the hole and standing up in the room now, full of menace. It would put out the light first. Already the flame in the lantern was trembling and flickering. The flame leapt and died. Darkness rushed in. And now the thing was moving towards him. He wanted to ward it off with a lighted stick, but he could not move his hand. With a great effort, he struggled with his tongue and said "White bird". He said it louder. As he spoke the words for the third time, it seemed as if the tower was falling in. There was a roll of confused sound, a thunderous noise and a cry – not his own. Something fell away into the ruin and was buried under falling stones, deep, immeasurably deep, beneath the earth.

He woke in terror, sweating in spite of the cold. Was it a dream he had had? The room was filled with a dim grey light coming in through the windows. It must be dawn. But the lantern was not alight. It had gone out. Something had happened. As his dull mind struggled to understand, there was another violent noise, the noise he had heard in his dream. It came from underneath. Someone was hammering on the tower door. He heard a distant, loud, insistent voice. "Open the door, in the name of the king!"

He started up. The king had come. But the lantern was out. He had kept it alight all night, only to fail at the end. What would Aelf and her father say? What would the king do, the king who flogged the keepers who let their lights go out? But he would have to answer, as he had to answer when his stepfather asked where he was. Trembling, he made his way down the ladder, pulled hard at the ring at the back of the door and heaved it open.

He found himself facing a nobleman with a large moustache, dressed in a riding cloak, with a sword belt under it. Eddi knew what to do when you met an angry man. He put his hands up to his face.

The nobleman spoke. "Are you the keeper of the light? The king wishes to see you. Come now and meet him."

He waited for the blow, but no blow came. Perhaps he was meant to confess first. "Lord, it is all my fault," he cried. "I let the light go out. I tried to look after it all, but I fell asleep."

The nobleman looked at him. "You must talk to Alfred, our king. Come now." He took a pace back to allow Eddi to come out. Eddi dropped his arms and looked through the door. The world outside had changed. The lane beside the tower was full of men and horses. Dozens of them. Campfires were alight, amid the snow. Meat was being roasted on sticks. Hay was being given to horses.

The nobleman beckoned to him to follow and led him down the lane, round the corner to Wade's house. Eddi saw in terror that there was a guard of armed men outside it. The nobleman pushed through the doorway and Eddi followed him. Inside, the hall was full of people. Aelf was there. "Eddi," she said, "the king saw the light!"

He looked down, ashamed and not knowing what to say. Then he heard a voice: deep yet reassuring. "Come here." He turned and saw a figure sitting on a chair, with men standing round him. The figure was a man, in a rich robe, with an enamelled jewel hanging from his neck. He was a man in his late forties, his beard touched with grey. His face was strong and wise and kind. It was the king.

Eddi fell on his knees and bowed his head.

"Wade's daughter tells me that you kept the light last night, because her father was sick and she looked after him," said the king.

"I tried to, lord," said Eddi, "and I did for most of the night. But then I fell asleep and the light went out. Lord, forgive me for failing. And spare this house, it was not their fault."

"What is this?" said the king. "The light out? It was not out when we crossed the marshes. It was still dark when we came and we saw the light in the distance. We steered towards it and

we found the ford. You have done well. We have seen other
places on our way, where the lights are not kept. You and your
master's family have done us faithful service. We are grateful."

"My father lights the lantern every night," said Aelf, "but last
night we knew that it was specially important, because we heard
you were coming." She told the king how they had found the
white bird, with the message round its foot.

"This is surprising," said the king. He turned to the
nobleman. "Odda, we sent no word of our coming, did we?"

"No, lord," said the nobleman. "For we came very quickly.
And we do not usually send birds with messages, but riders on
horseback."

The king thought for a moment. "God speaks to us through
birds," he said. "It is said by wise men that our life is like a bird
flying into a room from the darkness and out again. And the
spirit of God was seen, like a bird, when our Lord Jesus went
into the river to be baptised. In seeing a bird, perhaps you saw
the Spirit of God, coming to stir you up to do good works. And
if your light went out, perhaps the Spirit took its place and gave
out its own brightness. We too need the help of the Spirit, for we
are riding to London to lead the people against the Danes who
have landed again. It is an encouraging thought that the Spirit
may be flying with us. Now, let us have breakfast. In half an hour,
we must be on our journey. You shall have breakfast too and tell
me about your family while we eat."

There was much bustling round the fire, as old Hilda and the
king's cook competed to prepare bread and roast meat for
breakfast and warmed the ale to put into the king's cup and
wooden cups for Aelf and Eddi. Meat and ale were taken into

the bedroom for Wade, who had woken much refreshed from
his night's sleep.

When breakfast was over, the king went into the bedroom
and spoke to the farmer. Then he came out and called to the
nobleman, "Wade fought for us against the Danes."

The nobleman nodded. "Yes, sir, he was wounded."

"I want you to give him a command here and more land,"
said King Alfred. "Then he can organise the local men and help
defend the district. Please arrange this, Odda, and report to us
that it has been done." The nobleman bowed. "And this village
should not have a ruined church. See that timber is got and that
the men of the village repair the walls and put on a roof. And
find a piece of land here, on which a priest can live and get his
living. The tower should be a light for the Lord, not just for
travellers."

Aelf fell on her knees. The king smiled. "This is Twelfth Day –
the day when the kings rode to see the Christ child. It is a good
day for a king to bring a gift. And now," he said, "we too must
ride and ride fast towards London." He thanked them
courteously and left with his men.

When Wade had got over the shock of entertaining the king, he
called in Eddi and said, "You helped to change our fortune. You
shall share it."

Aelf hugged Eddi and Hilda said to him, "You're a bringer of
good luck!" Eddi's face was hot with embarrassment. Hilda then
remarked, "There's one good thing about it all. You won't have
to bother with that old light again."

"Why ever not?" asked Aelf.

"Well, kings don't come here more than once in a hundred years, so you are safe for a long time now."

Aelf laughed, but later that day, when it grew dark, she and Eddi went back up the tower with a fresh candle.

Chapter 2

THE MONK AND THE MILLER'S POOL

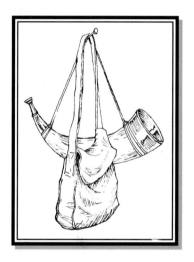

A stone splashed into the river. Another followed, and a third. The boy who was throwing them sat on the top of a cliff, some twenty feet above the passing water. His sister stood nearby, watching a cow and half a dozen sheep which were grazing on the hill behind the cliff. It was a warm sunny day in early March. Celandines showed yellow in the grass and the wild daffodils were out. Beside the hill a thin smoke rose in the air from a cottage, hidden in a dell. This was where the boy and girl lived.

The boy was picking pebbles out of the soil and trying to throw them right across the river. The girl, after giving another glance at the animals, sat down and rested her arms and chin on her knees. Ahead of her, a little to the right, the roofs and smoke of Brierleigh village showed through the trees. A road led from the village towards her, passing the cliff top about a hundred yards away on the right hand side. There was a horseman on the road, coming in her direction. She could not see who it was, and soon the rider was hidden by trees.

The boy got to his feet to throw more effectively. He pitched another stone and gave a shout. "Got it!" The girl looked up and, as she did so, her eyes caught a movement from the road. The figure on horseback was now level with them. It was a man in black with a pointed hood on his head.

"Get down, Ulf," she said urgently. "It's the Monk."

The boy turned round and looked, before moving rather slowly behind a tree. "So what?" he said. "He won't be coming here."

There was indeed no reason why he should. The Monk was their enemy; they were his victims. It was ten years since Wulfnoth, the lord of the manor, had ridden off to fight for King Harold at Hastings and had never come back. Now, there was a new Norman king and a new Norman lord, William de Treminet. "William Three Minutes" people called him. That was as long as it took him to seize your land, cut down the crop, and drive off the animals. He came to the village only for brief periods, staying with his men in the manor house and eating all the food he could get from the villagers. With him came this monk, who was his agent. The Monk turned up more often than the lord – once a week or so – giving orders. Who he was, where he lived, and why he was not in a monastery, were mysteries. He could speak English well, but he seemed to be a foreigner and most people feared him, for he always came with demands.

A few men in the village, however, saw the Monk as an ally and a way of growing rich. Gyrth, a fat and loud-mouthed peasant, was particularly servile and grovelling. He won the Monk's confidence and was made reeve, or headman, of the village. One day, soon afterwards, Gyrth came to the children's parents' house, a pleasant farm in the centre of the village, and said that the Monk had given it to him. There was no way of resisting. The family had to move out and feel lucky that Gyrth allowed them to occupy a tumbledown cottage by the river.

So why should the Monk call where he would not be welcome? Ulf walked back to the cliff edge and went on throwing stones. Goda, his sister, drew up her knees again and looked into the distance. But then there was a noise of snapping twigs. Footsteps sounded, hollow on the path. The bushes hissed, as somebody pushed through. Suddenly, the black-

hooded figure emerged beside them, on the top of the hill.
Goda froze; Ulf turned round with a stone in his hand.

"Go on with your throw," said a voice from inside the hood.
Ulf hesitated. "Go on, throw it." Ulf threw out his hand and the
stone flew over the river, landing well on the other side.

"You are a good thrower," said the voice. The hood turned
towards Goda. "And you," it said, "what can you do?" Goda
blushed. She didn't answer.

"You watch the sheep," said the voice. "You watched me
coming, too, didn't you? You told your brother to hide. I need
good throwers and watchers. I serve the lord and the lord serves
the king. The king needs throwers in his army and women to
watch his lands when the men are away. I can get you into his
service."

They both said nothing. He sat down on the grass beside
them, throwing back his hood upon his shoulders. His hair was
also black and hung down to his neck. There was no sign of a
circle cut on the top, like monks had. His face was sunburnt and
his jaws were covered by a growth of black stubble. His robe was
belted at the waist with a girdle of thick black rope, with two
hanging ends. Apart from this, there was nothing especially
monkish about him. He looked at the boy, and then at the girl.

"You don't like me, do you?" he said. "You blame me because
you are here. But it was not my fault – I had nothing to do with
it. Gyrth asked the lord. If you serve me, I can get you a good
farm in the village, as good as the farm you lost." Goda thought
to herself, "Why does he need our service?" She looked away.

The Monk took down a bag from his shoulder. "Have a cake,"
he said. He poured out some small, round golden cakes on the
grass. "Go on, have one."

Ulf took a cake suspiciously, and tasted it. His face changed. He took a larger bite. "It's good," he said. The cake was sweet and had a spicy flavour. He ate it quickly.

"Have another," said the Monk. "And you – what is your name?"

"Goda," she said.

"Goda, a very good name," he said. He stressed the word "good", sarcastically she felt. "And what is your brother called? Ulf? An ordinary Saxon name. I shall call him Wolf. Wolf is a wilder, stronger sort of name. Have a cake, good little Goda."

"No thank you," she said, "I am not hungry."

"Not hungry for my cakes? Have a stone then." He picked up a pebble and tossed it into her lap. "Wolf will have another – here, Wolf." Ulf took the cake and ate it.

"I've told you," said the Monk, "I am looking for men and women, boys and girls, to serve my lord. You can throw stones, Wolf – can you use a sling?"

"Yes," said Ulf.

"And a bow?"

"I've got a bow," said the boy eagerly, "and I can shoot a hundred yards."

"I will make you a soldier," said the Monk. "There is a world out there to be won." He pointed across the river towards the horizon. "People who stay here are peasants. They grow fat, like Gyrth. But strong men, Wolf, go out into the world. Out there are kings and nobles and battles. There is plunder to bring home and buy manors and men to serve you. Out there, Goda, are men to give you golden chains and bracelets. Why don't you look up? Come into my service. I will see your parents about it – but not now."

He turned his face again towards the river. "They say the water is very deep here – is that true?"

"Yes," said Ulf. "I can swim the river, but I can't dive to the bottom. The deepest part is over by the road. They call it the Miller's Pool."

"Come down and show me," said the Monk. He stood up, slinging his bag across his shoulder. Ulf made to follow him. Goda stayed where she was.

"You too," said the Monk, waving his hand. "The cow can look after itself." She went after them slowly.

The path down to the road was steep and there was one point where you had to climb over a rock. Ulf leapt down it, showing off, with outstretched arms. The Monk made an agile jump, but Goda paused. She did not want to do the same as the others. The Monk looked back as if he guessed her feelings. He turned his face towards her, with its faint sneer – she thought. "Jump down," he said, "and I'll catch you."

She lowered her eyes. "No thank you," she said and climbed down carefully. The Monk shrugged and walked on.

They came out on to the road. "Where is this Miller's Pool?" he asked again. The children led the way along the road. It was like all the roads round about and ran between high, grassy banks topped with hedges. Near the river, however, there was a place where one of the banks had disappeared for several yards, undermined by the rushing water. This part of the road was dangerous, because the side by the river ended in a sharp drop of ten or fifteen feet, straight into the water. Passers-by and carts were only saved from slipping over by a kerb of large stones placed at the edge of the road.

Ulf pointed to the river running beneath. "That is the

Miller's Pool," he said. "It's hundreds of feet deep."

"Why is it called the Miller's Pool?" asked the Monk, who seemed interested in everything.

Ulf was silent. He did not know. Goda found herself unwillingly explaining. "One night, years ago," she said, "a miller was driving his cart along the road. The river had worn the side away and it was open like it is now. The miller had had too much to drink and he was driving badly. The horse stumbled and the cart overturned. The miller fell into the river and was never seen again."

"A story with a moral," said the Monk, with a mocking smile.

"It's true," said Goda hotly. "He was carrying a millstone in his cart. The stone fell out and cracked. They used the bits to put along the side, to stop other people from falling over. The stones are still here." She pointed to them; they were hard and grey. Some of them had curved edges.

"We must be careful, Wolf," said the Monk, "and not come down here when we are drunk. Goda, I am sure, will never get drunk." He seemed to lose interest in the story. "Now I must go." He climbed on his horse. "I will see you again," he called, and galloped off along the road to the city.

They stood there for a while, staring after him. Goda said, "I don't like him."

Ulf said, "Why not? He was friendly enough – he could do us some good." But Goda hoped that nothing more would happen.

Some days went by, days of fine spring weather. Then, one afternoon, Goda returned from the village to find her parents talking excitedly. The Monk had called. He had told them that he wished to do them good and give them a better farm. He had promised to help their children to enter the lord's service. Goda tried to say that she did not like the Monk, but this was badly received.

"He's an important man," said her father. "He'll make our fortune for us. We're going to do what he wants, and that means all of us – including you, my girl. As soon as the lord comes back, the Monk will take you to see him – and mind you curtsy!"

When the lord returned, the children were told to present themselves at the manor. They went, one afternoon. The lord and his men had been out hunting and sat in the great hall with their boots on, quaffing wine. Goda found it hateful to be there. The lord was in a carved chair, looking like an eagle with his narrow eyes and hooked nose. The Monk introduced them, speaking French. The lord looked closely at them and replied. When he finished, there was a roar of laughter. The Monk smiled. He told them to bow and curtsy, then led them away.

Outside, he said to Ulf, "You have done well. The lord has decided to try you out in his service."

"When?" asked Ulf.

"Straightaway. Come here tomorrow morning, with your clothes. You will sleep here, in the stable loft, but you can go home sometimes for an hour or two, when things are quiet."

Goda said, "What about me?" She dreaded that a job had been found for her.

The Monk put on a mocking expression. "You don't want to work here, do you? I could see how icy and disapproving you were. The lord has no plans for you yet, but he will have some in a year or two. He said that the boy can work for him now, and he will have the girl when she is older. In the meantime, you must just stay at home and be good."

Goda was relieved at this and her parents were overjoyed at the news. With the favour of the Monk and with Ulf in the lord's service, they felt they had outwitted Gyrth and were well on the way to recovering their old farm, or another as good. The rest of the day was spent in packing Ulf's clothes, making him a better belt and finding him a knife to cut his food.

The next day, Ulf walked proudly down the road to enter the lord's service. When he got to the manor, he was put to carrying logs, bringing in hay to the stables and cleaning them out. There were eight other boys at the hall and three of them slept in the stable loft. The food was plentiful and there was often time between tasks to play fivestones together or throw stones at a target.

The Monk was often away, sometimes for days. His comings and goings were always unpredictable, but when he was at home he would watch the boys for a few moments, as if he was sizing them up. Every week or so, he made them practise archery or wrestling for an hour or two, or play football. Once, he taught them a game called "lying". It was a game in which you were questioned and had to tell lies about where you had been, or what you had in your hand. When Ulf came home, he boasted about these games, and told how the Monk would teach them tricks to win. Goda disliked his boasting and thought the tricks were dishonest. It seemed that you could tamper with arrows, making them shoot a little to one side, which you knew and your opponent didn't. You could twist your enemy's arm while wrestling, or jab your knee at him to loosen his hold. Football was even better, because it was rough and all sorts of fouls were possible. This was Ulf's favourite game and he played it whenever he could.

After Ulf had been at the manor for a few weeks, the lord announced that he and his men were going to France, where he had other lands. But before he left, because the people had been obedient and had done what he wanted in three minutes, he said he would give them a May Day entertainment on the village meadow. His men would show their skill at fighting on foot and jousting on horseback. There would be wrestling by the village men, with a ram as the prize, and a football match between the boys of Brierleigh and the next village. The boys' prize was to be a Saxon horn, decorated with silver. It was part of the lord's plunder at the battle of Hastings and he intended to give it to whoever scored the most goals.

The day was fine and the meadow was crowded. There were stalls selling cakes and ale. There were musicians and pedlars and even a juggler. Goda sat with her parents on the grass, watching the fighting and jousting. At last a horn blew and the football players ran on to the field, to the sound of loud cheering. It was a ragged, violent game, with two or three dozen boys on either side and the two trainers (the Monk and a farmer from the next village) urging on their teams. Goda thought that the boys played roughly, especially in the Monk's team. They thrust and punched, and kicked out with large boots which the Monk had given them. Ulf scored, pushing his way through by force. The team from the other village was faster and wore lighter boots. Their leader was a slim boy with fair hair. He caught the ball and darted away with it. Ulf ran up to intercept him. The boy kicked the ball deftly past Ulf and ran away with tremendous speed. He scored in the Brierleigh goal and his own side waved their arms and cheered. Ulf stamped his boots on the grass with anger.

The ball was put back in the middle and the two sides struggled for it. The fair-haired boy got it again and made to go round the outside of the field. Ulf ran up to him, and for a moment the ball lay between them. Goda, watching, saw Ulf give a savage kick: not at the ball but at the other boy's ankle. The boy fell down in pain and Ulf took the ball, driving it on and on and into the goal. His own team shouted, punched the air and jeered their opponents. There was a tremendous cheer from the lord's men and the Brierleigh villagers. Hands waved mugs of ale. Nobody seemed to have noticed the foul, or to be bothered about it if they had. The beaten team gathered round the wounded boy and sullenly carried him off. The Monk shouted congratulations and smacked Ulf on the shoulder.

The lord had watched the games from a chair on a platform. He held a large cup on his lap, which was filled for him from time to time by a servant. He called out, and the Monk brought Ulf before the lord and told him to kneel. Ulf knelt and the lord looked keenly at his face. He lifted the cup, spoke and drank deeply.

"He drinks to you," said the Monk. "Now bow your head."

Ulf did so. The lord gave another order, and the servant brought him the horn. He spoke again in French and put the horn into Ulf's hands.

"He gives it to you," said the Monk. "Put your hands between his and reply, 'mon seigneur'. That means that you accept him as your lord."

Ulf put his hands up, and the lord closed his around them; the hands felt hard and cold. Ulf said the words and the lord smiled with his thin lips.

"Now bow again," said the Monk, "and go. You are no longer a boy. He has made you one of his men because you have done well."

Ulf left the lord's side and came racing across the field with the horn. His parents rose to greet him and others gathered round, fingering the horn and praising Ulf. Even Gyrth, who was lounging in a chair nearby, called for the boy to show him the lord's gift and swore that the goals were good ones. Goda felt angry at this. She had seen what happened during the match and did not think that Ulf had won the horn at all fairly. How could everyone pretend it did not matter? She sat there silent and unnoticed as the merrymaking went on until the afternoon began to draw into evening. Ulf went back to the stables and Goda's parents prepared to go home. Goda went with them.

As Ulf entered the stable yard, the Monk drew him aside. "I am pleased with you today, Wolf. You have learnt my lessons well. You are tough and can get what you want. Now I have something important for you to do. It means that you will have to go away for about a month, so tonight you can go home and say goodbye to your family. Tell them that you are leaving for Winchester tomorrow for the lord, but warn them not to say so to anyone else. Your mission is secret."

He dipped his hand into a pocket and brought out a bag. "Tell me about your sister Goda," he said. "Does she love you?"

Ulf looked surprised. "Yes, I suppose she does," he said.

"Would she keep a secret if you asked her?"

"She would if I told her to," said Ulf.

"I want you to take this bag," said the Monk. "It is full of silver coins. They belong to the lord. When you do business for him, you may want money. I shall not always be here. This money is for you to keep at home. It will be safer there. Your sister must look after it and hide it, then you can use it whenever you need.

Again, nobody else must know about this – not even your parents – and you must swear her to secrecy."

"Am I to take it now?" asked Ulf.

"Yes," said the Monk. "Take it now. Leave the money at home with your sister tonight and come and see me early tomorrow morning, ready to travel. I shall give you detailed orders then."

Ulf took the bag and bowed. He slung the horn across his shoulder and walked home, full of elation. People from the village cheered him as he passed. He got back to the house and said to his mother, "Where's Goda?"

"She's up on the hill."

He went out, holding the bag. He found her sitting by the cliff edge, looking out at the darkening sky. "I didn't see you at the games," he said.

"No," she said shortly.

"You haven't seen my horn."

"No."

She sat looking straight ahead. Her silence irritated him.

"Well, everyone else thought it was good," he said. "Everyone praised me – even Gyrth. They were glad that I won."

"Did you kick that boy on purpose?" she said.

Ulf laughed. "Yes. I hurt him," he said. "I hate him."

"Is that sporting?" she asked.

"Yes," he said, "in order to win. I wanted to win, and I did."

Goda said, "Is that what the Monk has taught you?"

Ulf said, "He teaches us to win. I am going to be a soldier and in battle it's winning that counts. You have to be ruthless."

She said, "I don't think that is right."

Ulf nearly lost his temper. He remembered, just in time, that he needed her help.

"All right," he said, "we don't agree. It doesn't matter. Look, I want you to do something for me."

"What do you want?"

"I'm going away tomorrow, on business for the lord. I want you to look after this bag. You must keep it safely and secretly, without telling anyone." He put down the bag beside her. She looked at it.

"What's inside?"

He opened the neck of the bag. It was half full of round silver coins with kings' faces on them. They gleamed in the evening light.

"Where did you get this money?" she asked.

"The Monk gave it to me. He wants you to keep it for me, in a secret place, so that I can use it when I need to."

She felt a trap. She knew the Monk did not like her. Why was he going to trust her with this money? Suppose people came and said it was stolen?

"No," she said. "I don't want to. It's too valuable. I can't look after anything as precious as this."

He argued with her. "The Monk told me to ask you. It belongs to the lord."

"Well, if the lord asks me to, I will."

"We can't ask the lord," he said. "He's going away." She said nothing. He made a last attempt. "Please do it. For me. It's to help me rise in the lord's favour."

"And the Monk's favour?" she said. "Like kicking people?"

Ulf looked furious. "You don't love me, and you haven't done ever since I went into the lord's service."

Goda said, "That's not true."

He said, "I'm not spending my life watching sheep in a field.

All right. Stay here and live in a cottage, if you want to. I don't care."

He turned and marched back to the house. When she came home, he was telling his father about his journey for the lord. His mother was bustling about, finding clothes to put in his bag. He ignored Goda for the whole of the evening.

Next morning, she followed him down the path to the road. "Ulf," she said, "I am sorry we quarrelled. I love you and I want you to be safe. I will pray for you, until you come back."

"I don't need your prayers," he said. "I can look after myself." He put the bag on his shoulder, pushed through the hedge and strode off. He did not turn his head. She thought, with bitterness, "The Monk has won again."

When Ulf reached the manor house, it was empty. The lord had taken most of his men away and the few who were left were out at work in the fields. The Monk called Ulf into his room. Ulf gave him back the bag. "I am sorry, sir," he said. "My sister was afraid to look after it." The Monk raised his eyebrows and put on his mocking expression.

"What! The good Goda would not care for it, even for you!" He seemed amused. "It doesn't matter. I want to tell you what you are going to do."

He pointed to a heap of dirty clothes. "Put these on, so that you look like a poor boy, and go to a castle about thirty miles from here. Not Winchester; a place called Falconbury. When you arrive there, say you are looking for work. The servants will ask you who you are, and you must tell them lies. Say that your name is … Gyrth. That's a name you know well, and do not say that you come from here. Do you know any other village?"

"Yes," said Ulf, "we have cousins at Asherton and I have been there to stay."

"Good. Say that you come from Asherton and that you are your cousin's son. They will give you work in the kitchen or somewhere. While you are there, you must find out all you can about the castle – the plan, the gates, the towers, the stairs, how many men there are. The lord of the castle is plotting against the king. Listen to people talking and remember what they say. When you have been there for a month, come home. But you must slip away carefully and travel at night, in case you are traced. When you get back, the lord will reward you richly. He will take away Gyrth's farm and give it back to your father. Gyrth is fat and lazy. Your father would make a better headman too."

It took Ulf the rest of that day and part of the next to walk to Falconbury. At first, the great adventure went very well. He arrived at the castle, asked for work and was given a job in the woodyard. This was a good job for a spy. He was sent all over the place with fuel for fires and wood for carpenters. He listened to conversations. He found where the lord of the castle lived, and one afternoon, when he had been there nearly a month, he saw that the room was empty. He looked to see if anyone was watching and went in. There was a bed, chairs, a table – a letter on the table. He picked it up and tried to read it.

It was a pity that the lord's servant came back suddenly. Ulf was caught in the room. He was taken before the lord and interrogated. At first, Ulf would say nothing, even when the lord hit him in the face. But then the lord's men twisted his arms very painfully. He cried out and confessed that he came from Brierleigh and that his master was the Monk. The lord was interested by this, so interested that he sat down and began to write a letter about it to somebody else. He looked up, and merely ordered the boy to be flogged and thrown out of the castle. The lord's men were even kinder; they just beat him up and kicked him all over. Then they carried him into the road.

When they had gone, he crawled into some bushes. He cried a little, thinking of what he would say when he had to confess to the Monk. At last, night came and he started to make his way home. His bruises were painful and his right foot was swollen where a boot had caught his ankle. That night he only covered a few miles. He slept for most of the next day and begged some bread from a woman in a cottage. He drank from the streams that he crossed. The third day he reached Brierleigh, but he was afraid to be seen, ragged and lame as he was. He watched the men at work on the land and hid until they went home. In the early evening, he came down by a backway into the lord's manor.

As he entered the stable yard, the Monk was crossing it. The Monk looked round swiftly, and beckoned Ulf into his room. He shut the door, sat in a chair, and pointed to the floor. Ulf crouched down and began to stammer his tale: how he had been discovered, tortured and made to say where he came from. The Monk looked at him closely. As the story went on, he turned his face away and fingered his girdle. He tied a loop in one of the hanging cords and pulled it tight. At the end, he remarked, "I am surprised, Wolf. I thought you knew how to tell lies." That was all.

He was silent for a while, then he said, "You had better rest here for a little. I will take you home later." He went out for several minutes and came back with a wooden cup. He gave it to

Ulf and said, "Here is some wine to make you better." Ulf sat on the floor and sipped the wine – it tasted rich and spicy, like the cakes. He drank it, wishing it were not so sweet. Then he felt tired. He put down the cup and rested his back against the wall. His head fell forward.

The Monk, who had been watching, lifted the boy in his arms and carried him out of the room. He dragged Ulf over the deserted yard and into a shed, laid the boy on the floor and locked the door. His plans had gone badly wrong. The boy had been discovered and the Falconbury men would be able to trace him. Important people would ask what the Monk was doing and for whom he was spying. He himself could bluff the matter out, but the boy must disappear – there must be no witness to what had been going on. He thought of how he could take Ulf away. He would have to wait until midnight. In fact, he would wait until an hour or two afterwards, in case anyone was up late on a June summer night. Then he would go down to the river. He remembered that first day, and the deep pool. He had often looked at it since.

Late that afternoon, when Goda was in the village, running an errand for her mother, she saw a farmworker coming out of a lane. He shouted at her, "How's your brother Ulf?"

"Ulf's still away," she told him, "doing work for the lord. We don't know when he's coming back."

"He's back already," said the man. "I was working up in Stenson copse this afternoon, and I saw him go past down the hedges. Limping, he was. Not like he runs when he's playing football. I thought maybe the boy had hurt himself."

This strange news troubled her. she thanked the man, and

went on to her home. "Perhaps he will be there when I come," she thought, but he was not. She told her parents what she had heard, but did not mention the limping. They took the news calmly. Her father said, "He will go to the lord's first. He will come tomorrow if he is here." But Goda felt worried. Why should he come back limping through the fields? If he had returned after such a long absence, it was strange that he had not come down to see his parents. The lord was still away and there was little work at the hall. She thought again about their quarrel, and realised that she and her parents had no knowledge of what he had been doing. He might have been in danger, with only her prayers to support him.

It was late when she got to sleep and she did not sleep for long. She woke up suddenly. It was still deep night, but a full moon shone in at the window. She tried to sleep again, but couldn't. She decided to dress and get up. It was a warm night, and dawn would be early. When daybreak came, she could go up to the manor. She put on her clothes and left the house softly, closing the door behind her. Then she climbed on to the hill to look out over the landscape. At first the world seemed altogether still, except for the rushing of the river. Then, after a little, her ears – used to the silence – picked up another noise: the hooves of a horse in the road.

She felt an urge to see who was going by so early in the morning. She slid down the big rock and slipped through the gap in the hedge, out into the road. The road itself was dark inside its deep hedge banks, but ahead of her lay the part of it that ran above the Miller's Pool. This part, being open on the left-hand side, was bathed in a brilliant light from the moon as it set in the west of the sky. As she approached, she could see a rider stop his horse in the patch of moonlight. He was a large, hooded shape upon his mount. It was the Monk. He swung himself down from the horse and fastened its reins to a small branch in the hedge opposite the drop down to the river, a few yards in front of her. From the back of the horse he lifted a large bundle, a heavy bundle which gave him some trouble to hold. As he struggled to put it down, she saw that it was the body of a boy. For a moment, the face caught the light. It was her brother's face; the eyes were closed.

The Monk laid the boy in the road and went back to the horse. He took a bag from beside the saddle and bent over, picking up stones and putting them into the bag. It would have to be heavy enough to weigh down the boy, when he threw him into the water.

The trouble was that there were no big stones. He looked round and remembered the pieces of millstone by the edge of the cliff. He stood up, tugged at one, pulled it out and staggered with it to the bag. He did the same with a second and a third. Three heavy pieces of millstone would be more than enough to sink a body right to the bottom of the river.

The boy on the ground stirred a little and moved his arm. Goda felt her heart beat – he was still alive. The Monk, having filled his bag, considered how to tie it to the body. He looked on the horse's back for the rope he had brought, but could not find it. Perhaps it had fallen off. However, that was no problem; he could use his thick rope girdle. He squatted down by the cliff edge and tied one end to his bag. Then he took out his knife to cut the girdle. Goda felt what he was going to do, rather than understood it, and ran forward. Her movement startled the horse. It shrieked with fear, reared up, and tried to turn. It tore its reins from the branch, wheeled round and galloped off. As it passed beside the Monk, one hind leg hit him on the head. He put up his arm to ward it off and lost his balance. He fell forwards over the edge of the cliff, dragging the bag by his girdle after him. There was an exclamation, a splash as he reached the water and a thump as the bag landed on top of him. For a brief moment, his clothes held him up and he struggled, but the bag pushed him under and went down with him, right down to the bottom of the river. The sound of the galloping horse died away in the distance. Silence fell.

Goda ran up to the cliff edge and looked down. The pool lay sparkling in the moonlight, but all she saw were the ripples of the current, as the river flowed across the deeps below. The Monk had gone: his horse had gone – as if they had never been there. She turned to the boy. Again, he stirred. As far as she could see, he was not tied up or hurt: it was as if he was waking from a sleep. She cradled his head in her arms and kissed his forehead. He opened his eyes and saw her, and his eyes filled with tears. "I am so sorry, so sorry," he whispered. After a few minutes, he was able to walk, with her support, back to the house.

At Goda's suggestion, Ulf reported for work next day at the manor. He told his parents that he had been beaten by soldiers – which was true. He half expected to see the Monk at the manor house, but the Monk was not there. Nobody knew where he was. His horse had been found in the stable yard, saddled as if for a journey. Some days passed. A messenger came from the lord, anxious to see the Monk, and rode away angrily when he could not be found. After this, a rumour started in the village that the Monk was in trouble and had fled abroad to France. Goda, having looked again at the roadside and seen that three pieces of millstone were missing, thought differently.

Later that summer, Gyrth died unexpectedly after eating a whole roast pig at a wedding party. Another headman was appointed, and he put the parents of Ulf and Goda back into their old farm in the village. Ulf got permission to leave the lord's service and joined his father on the farm. Goda liked all this, but most of all she was glad not to have to walk along the road beside the river. The cliffside there is dangerous, and it is very deep in the Miller's Pool.

Chapter 3

THE WAY TO JERUSALEM

"Battles, I can understand," said the Lady Juliana, biting into a large and succulent piece of chicken. She paused and swallowed a mouthful. "Pilgrimages are pathetic!"

It was dinner time in the hall of the manor house. The Lady was sitting at the head of the table. Thomas, the ancient butler, looked ahead mournfully from behind her chair. Will, the kitchen boy, who was helping to carry the dishes, stifled a giggle. His friend John, who was sitting beside the Lady, looked at him and winked.

"A boy of your age," said the Lady Juliana, "should be interested in hunting and shooting. All this religion! Your father would have been most disappointed in you." She cut into the chicken with her knife. "He went to church regularly, of course he did. Christmas and Harvest. Then he was out with the hounds, when there wasn't a war on. If you want some excitement, why can't you join in a rebellion, or something?"

John had heard his mother on this subject ten or twenty times since he had told her about the pilgrimage. Every May, a company of pilgrims went from London to Jerusalem. John had decided to join them. Will the kitchen boy would come as his personal servant. They would be away for about eight months, and back in time for Christmas if they were lucky.

The Lady Juliana was not pleased. A pilgrimage to Jerusalem, dodging robbers and sailing across the seas in a leaky boat, was not her style at all. Why couldn't John take her on a nice English pilgrimage to Canterbury, with a week or two shopping in London? She might find a new husband – people often did. Instead of which, the boys were going off on this ridiculous journey: tomorrow, in fact, the first of May. What nonsense!

The table was crowded with dishes. The lady of the manor liked good food. There were home-made rolls from the bakehouse, a big joint of beef with mustard sauce, two chickens, some roast ducks and a plate of fried larks. The Lady ate largely of everything, and wiped her lips on her napkin. Then she sprang her surprise.

"Well, if you must go, there's no more to be said. But I can't have you two boys leaving home without somebody to look after you. I've got you a companion." She saw John look at her intently, and she paused, enjoying the suspense. "The vicar is coming as well!"

John's jaw dropped and it was all that Will could do to stop himself from crying, "Oh, no!" The vicar! The pilgrimage was meant to be their own adventure, away from the grown-up people round them. The vicar was the last person they would have thought of taking. Looking after them! They would have to spend all their energies looking after him! The Vicar of Brierleigh was well known for miles around as the very vaguest vicar in the Church – the VVV for short. He would regularly ride northwards out of the village when he was going south. He sometimes said the morning service in the evening, and sometimes the other way round. At christenings, people stood round the font like fielders in case he dropped the baby. Even now, Will could see a label sticking up at the back of his collar. He was wearing something inside out.

The vicar put down the lark he was eating and beamed round the table. "It will be a pleasure to go with you," he purred. "I

have always wanted to see the Bethlehem shepherds and their
dear little lambs."

"We shall be riding very fast, sir," said John, in a rather
hopeless attempt to put the vicar off. He didn't feel he could
mention storms or robbers, having told his mother how safe the
journey would be. "And I'm afraid you'll find us rather noisy at
times."

"No trouble, no trouble at all," said the vicar, waving his hand
and dropping his lark in the sauceboat. "It is a pleasure to go
with you. And a splendid day to go, the first of May. "It's my
birthday. Oddly enough," he added, "It's my twin brother's
birthday as well." Will hastily covered his mouth with his hand.

"You will, of course, perform some jobs for me," said the
Lady, breaking in. "You can call in at Rome and tell the Pope to
bless my rosary. And I want a large bottle of water from the
Dead Sea. Lady Pyne has one on her window sill. She is always
showing it to people. Will! Have you found me a bottle?"

"I've got the big bottle of sherry you finished drinking this
morning, my lady," said Will, producing it from the sidetable.
The Lady frowned.

"That will do, Will. Make sure you don't forget it. And now,
Thomas, I think if the vicar has really finished with the larks, you
can bring in the puddings."

Early next morning, Will trudged out of his mother's cottage
towards the church – the place, according to the pilgrimage
rules, that you had to start from. On his back was an enormous
pack and he was ticking off items on his fingers. "Shirts, socks,
surcoat. Map of the world, tinderbox for lighting fires and three
sticks of liquorice." He turned into the church lane, and said,
"Gosh! Look at all the people."

John had intended leaving as quietly as possible. The Lady Juliana had decided otherwise. She had sent the bailiff round the village at dawn, banging on people's doors, and now a crowd of tenants and farm labourers, wives and children had gathered in the church lane to see the pilgrims set off. Some people were yawning, some were rubbing their eyes, and some were as mutinous as they dared to be, given that the Lady was present in her best and largest head-dress with her household servants around her.

"What's the point of travelling round the world?" said one. "Why don't he stay at home, and go hunting and pay us to go with him?"

"It's all to do with his honour," said another. "All the lords of Brierleigh must do great deeds. It's an exploit. When he comes back, we'll be top village. Put them Woodstoke folk in their places. They've never had no pilgrims."

The Lady's voice rang out. "Your lord and vicar are leaving you on pilgrimage. Give them a cheer and say a prayer for their safe return."

John and the vicar were already mounted. Will scrambled on to his pony. A ragged cheer went up. There was a cry, "They're off!"

Will thought, "They think it's a race. The Jerusalem cup." He pressed his pony with his heels and it moved into a fast trot. John's horse began to trot as well and the vicar swayed unsteadily after them. There was another cheer and a sound of blowing horns. The riders turned the corner, waving goodbye. Their last sight was the Lady, standing majestically in front of the crowd.

Three months later, John sat on a low wall in the sun, waiting for Will to join him. They had reached the edge of the Alps. Ahead, the mountains reared up huge and grey, with white streaks of snow on their heads. He thought about the journey so far. Things had not gone smoothly. First, there was the delay at Southampton, when the ships refused to sail because of the war. Then in France they had run into the plague. The roads were closed and they were stuck in a small town for a month. Last of all, there was the vicar. He stubbed his toe in one town, lost himself in another and got an upset stomach in a third. Time and money were running out. If they did not reach Venice in two weeks, they would miss the last boat to Jerusalem. And now the vicar was missing again.

Will, who was searching the inn where they spent the night, rushed out. "He's made a mistake again, master," he panted. "The landlord says he paid his bill early this morning and went. We were in church, and the vicar thought we'd left. He's gone riding on to a place called St Bruno, about five miles away."

"Bother him!" said John. "I told him clearly last night that we were riding to St Bernard. He'll lose himself if we leave him. We'll have to ride to this Bruno place and find him. Perhaps they can tell us how to get to St Bernard and we can join the other pilgrims there."

They set out on their errand. The roads became steeper and narrower, and it took them an hour to reach St Bruno, a poor little tumbledown village. They found the inn and asked about the vicar.

"Ah, yes, the English priest," said the innkeeper, speaking French. "A very confused man. He stopped here for a cup of wine. He asked for pilgrims, and I told him that the pilgrims all go over the mountains through St Bernard, not this way. So he rode on. You will easily catch him up, for he rides slowly." He showed them the track they were to follow, up a valley. "But you must be on your guard," he added, "for they have had the plague in these parts. Very few people have been left alive."

The mountain track was stony. It wound beside a rushing stream through clumps of trees, with steep cliffs on each side. After a few miles the valley divided, and so did the track. There was no signpost and no one to ask. Will took out the map of the world, but it was quite useless for this purpose.

John looked at the sky to get a direction from the sun. But the sun was nowhere to be seen. Grey clouds drifted among the mountain peaks.

"We'll just have to try one way," said John, "and see if we come to a village. Then we can ask and go back if necessary, or hire a guide." They decided to go right. The track climbed steeply and left the stream below it. After a while, the valley grew broader. They could see fields in the distance and the roofs of a village. They stopped the horses and paused to look at the view. "Good," thought Will. "We can have a rest soon." But as they stopped, he felt a raindrop fall on his forehead. He suddenly noticed how dark it was. The clouds had gathered thick and low and there was a flicker of lightning. They were in for a storm.

They rode on, hoping to reach the village and shelter. But the rain came down in torrents. They were soon wet through. A sharp crack of thunder came close by, then another, making the horses shudder. They turned a corner and the cliff beside them ended. They entered a wide place, with a field or two and a thatched farmhouse and barn. "Let's go in there and ask for shelter," said John. They rode through the pelting rain and into the barn, through a large, open door. They dismounted and tied up the horses. No one came out to see them.

They sat on the floor for a long time, watching the rain outside. Large puddles of water formed upon the ground. They unpacked food and wine and had a meal. The storm raged for two hours, but gradually the thunder moved away and the rain slackened.

"Let's try the house, Will," said John. "We may find somebody and get directions." They pulled their hoods over their heads and walked across the yard to the house. Will knocked and called. There was no answer. He pushed open the door of the house and looked inside. Then he started back.

"There are bodies inside!" he cried. "Ghosts!"

"Nonsense, Will," said John, pushing past him. In the dim light, there were indeed the shapes of people sitting on the floor. He spoke in French. "Good day, good people. We are pilgrims, seeking directions to St Bernard."

A low voice came from one of the shadowy forms. "Ah, monsieur. This a poor house. We have nothing."

John opened the door to see things better. A man, a woman and some children were sitting or lying on the floor. Why did they not get up?

He spoke more loudly. "Can you tell us the way to St Bernard?"

Will had a sudden frightful thought. "The plague, master, beware! Perhaps they've got the plague."

The man who had spoken said something again. Will knew little French and did not understand what he was saying.

John did. "The man says he caught the plague, and could not work for a long time. They had to give their cows to the lord for rent and they sold their furniture. Now they have nothing. He says the plague has moved on, but they will die anyway."

"Let's go, then, master," said Will. "Let's try the village. We shan't find directions here."

To his surprise, John did not move. He remained standing, looking round the bare room, with its cold fireplace.

"These people are close to death from hunger, Will," said John. "If we leave them, they will die."

"Well, what are we supposed to do?" said Will irritably. He wanted to catch up the vicar and the other pilgrims.

"We must find them some food," said John. "What do we have in the bags?"

Will went to the barn to look. Presently he returned with a stick of bread and a bottle of water.

"Give it to the man," said John. "All right," as Will refused to enter the house. "I'll give it to him."

The man seemed to understand that he was being given food, but he shook his head. He pointed to the children. Will now saw that there were two small girls and an older boy. The man said a few words.

"He says we must feed the children first," said John. "I think we had better start with water and then a little bread. Not too much, if they have been starving."

He went into the room and gave the waterbottle to the two small children, then to the older boy. They sipped a little. Will tore the bread into pieces, and offered it to them. They began to chew. The mother and the father looked on, then they too received the water and the bread. The mother ate a little and clasped her hands.

"Dieu vous sauve, messieurs! Vous avez sauvé les vies."

John translated for Will. "She thanks God. She thinks we have saved their lives. But we have only just started. We must get them some proper food. You light a fire and I'll go down to the village." He spoke again to the parents. "Le village, est-il près d'ici?"

"Oui, monsieur. Au dessous de la colline," said the man.

"I'll take the horse and ride," said John. "Will, you make the fire."

Will found the next few hours difficult. He could not find any fuel and did not know how to ask where they kept it. The rain had stopped, so he went out collecting sticks, but everything he found was sopping wet. However, when he came back, the man had got up and seemed to realise what he was doing. The man shuffled out of the door, and pointed round the side of the house. In a corner, Will found a few, small, dry logs. He brought them in and made a fire with his tinderbox.

Presently, John came back from the village. He had found more bread, some wine, two rather skinny chickens and some vegetables. Will, as the expedition's professional cook, took charge of the food. He looked about for a pot. "There's nothing to cook it in, master," he said.

"As-tu un pot au feu?" asked John. The man reached up to a hole in the thatched roof, and pulled out an iron pot. He spoke in French.

"He says they had to hide it because the lord's men came searching to take things away," said John.

"The lords round here don't sound very nice!" said Will.

Within an hour or two a well had been discovered and a stew of chicken and vegetables was cooking on the fire. The inside of the house seemed lighter, partly with the fire, partly because the day was brightening into a clear summer evening. There was a good smell of food. The two small children stood up and started to run about.

Eventually, Will served supper. He and John had pieces of chicken, with bread. The family had stew from the pot and dipped their bread into it. A horn cup had been found into which John poured wine for the man and his wife. The boy pointed to his mouth when he saw this, and John refilled the cup for him.

"We shall have to stay here for the night now," said John. He explained this to the man, who jumped up, put his hand on his breast and offered them the hospitality of the house. "I think, however," John replied, "we'll sleep in the barn." He thought it wise because of the plague, and so that they could look after the horses and their bags in this unknown place.

They had a quiet night. Next morning, soon after dawn, they were woken by a noise. The two small girls had been out collecting daisies, and made chains. They came to the barn, and watched while John and Will woke up. They chattered, telling them to put on the chains.

The boys rose, went to the well and washed. John saw the man by the door of the house. The man bowed humbly, like a peasant to a lord. John said to him, in French, "Where do you work?"

The man's eyes filled with tears. "This is my holding," he said. "But all the cattle have been taken by the lord."

"Where is the lord?" asked John. It turned out that the lord himself lived several miles away in a castle, but his bailiff lived in the village. This was the man who had the cows.

John and Will ate more bread and wine in the barn for their breakfast, and discussed the situation. "There is no point in leaving them like this," said John. "They will starve again as soon as we go. We'll have to go to the village and buy back their cows."

"But we haven't got enough money," said Will. "We've only just enough to get to Jerusalem."

"It's more important to help them, Will," said John. "How can we go on to Jerusalem while there are people here who need our help?" Will looked discontented, but he did not say anything.

That day, John rode down to the village. The man, who was now stronger, walked beside his horse. Will stayed behind to look after the other horse and the bags. The woman was now able to move about. She collected wood and made up the fire. She sliced the vegetables and made another stew. The boy, who seemed about fifteen, came out of the house as well. He wandered over to the barn and looked at the horse and the bags. He spoke to Will. "Tu as monnaie?" he said. "Donne-moi monnaie."

Will caught the word "money". "I don't have money," he said. He did not altogether like the boy, who had a sharp, surly look. The boy lounged against the barn door, watching what Will was doing. After a while, he moved away.

In the afternoon, John came back. He brought more food: a whole sack of flour, a flask of oil, a cheese. He gave them to the woman and again she joined her hands in prayer. He explained to Will that he had bought back the cows. The bailiff had driven a hard bargain. It had cost several gold coins. But he had recovered three cows, which the man was driving home.

An hour or two later, the peasant returned. He put the cows into the cowshed and came and knelt in front of John. He offered thanks effusively – John was embarrassed. Later, the woman came over to the barn. She had cooked food, she said, and insisted that they should come and eat it by her fire. She had made cakes with flour and oil. They ate these with the family and had slices of the cheese. They shared wine. The small children chattered and ate, the boy munched greedily and asked for more. Once or twice, Will felt that the boy was watching him. When the meal was over, Will rose to feed the horses. The peasant intervened. "My son will go," he said. Will would have preferred to do the job himself, but John nudged him, as if to say that the family wanted to do something for them in return. So he sat where he was and soon the boy came back.

The sun set, and John and Will returned to the barn. "I think," said John, "that we will leave early tomorrow morning. I asked the way in the village. We should have turned left where we turned right, so we must go back down the valley. We won't say anything before we go; I don't want them to have to thank us. But with their cows back, they will be able to make another start in life."

Will agreed with relief. He felt uneasy and did not know why. He spread their cloaks on the ground to sleep on, with some hay underneath for pillows, and packed their other luggage ready for the morning. He felt the bags. One of them contained a purse of money. It was normally easy to feel the coins in the bag, but now he could not do so. He put his hand into the bag and found the purse. It was empty.

"Master, some of the money has gone!" he said in a low voice.

"Perhaps it has slipped into a corner," suggested John.

Will undid the bag and searched it thoroughly. "No," he said. "About a dozen silver coins have gone. I think it was the boy. He was looking at our things this afternoon and he was here on his own when he was feeding the horses."

"All the more reason for us to leave early in the morning," said John. "We are a temptation if we stay." He lay down on his cloak and went to sleep. Will lay down too, but resolved to stay awake and watch. In the end, however, he closed his eyes.

He was woken by John gently shaking him. It was already light. He roused himself and packed away their cloaks. They untied the horses and led them quietly through the yard. There was no sound from the farmhouse. It was a beautiful early morning. The sky was clear with the promise of sunshine, though the sun itself was still behind the mountains. They got on their saddles and rode down the track. On the left was a cliff leading down to the river below. On the right, a steep hillside rose up, covered with trees. The track was narrow, and they had to go carefully.

Suddenly Will, who was riding behind, felt something whizz past his head. There was a terrified scream from John's horse as a stone struck it in the side. It reared up. John had all he could do to keep his seat. "Ride on as fast as you can!" he shouted. "We're being attacked."

John's horse broke into an unsteady gallop down the track, while John held on as best he could. Will urged his mount in the same direction. A huge boulder shot down the hillside, crossed the track between their horses and fell down the cliff with a crash. Other stones followed, and one hit Will on the arm. He looked back and saw two figures hurling missiles. It was a miracle that neither horse stumbled or fell in their headlong flight, but somehow they galloped on. They rushed round a corner and along another wooded stretch until the track became wider and easier. "Don't stop yet," called John. "Get a couple of miles further." They managed to check the horses a little, however, and in twenty minutes they pulled up. They had reached the fork in the paths and they were both breathless.

"Was it the family?" said Will.

"I don't think so," said John. "They were grateful for what we did, I think. Even the boy was only tempted to steal. It's probably my fault. I spent money in the village and I asked the way, so people knew we were leaving. They must have been villagers, planning to rob us. It shows how dangerous it is in these out-of-the-way parts. Now, we'd better press on to St Bernard as quickly as we can."

Will was afraid that their attackers might know a secret way across the mountains and ambush them again. They rode for an hour uphill, looking out keenly for movements among the trees, until they came into a wide valley leading downwards. After a time, they were relieved to see the spire of a large church in the distance. It was St Bernard. They reached it, entered the village inn and had their horses fed and watered. They ordered breakfast.

"Monsieur is a pilgrim for Venice?" said the landlord, as he served them. "You are too late. The road is closed." The storm of two days ago was so heavy there, he told them, that a huge fall of rock had blocked the mountain pass. Their own party of pilgrims was the last to get through. Local men would work to reopen the road, but it would be a long job – a week or two, maybe three. They could go round by another pass, but that would take just as long.

"That settles it, Will," said John. "We can't go on. We've lost the other pilgrims. At least the vicar will be safe if he sticks with them. It's unsafe to travel through the mountains by ourselves, and even if we manage to reach the sea, we'll miss the last boat. We shall run out of money and have to beg for months before we get home. We must go back."

"But what about the Lady and her bottle?" asked Will anxiously. "Everyone's expecting us to get to Jerusalem and come back in triumph."

"They'll just have to be disappointed," said John. "Everything we've done has been right and sensible – we've been unlucky. But we've seen France and the mountains and we can come back another time."

"All right, master," said Will gloomily, "but I don't think that the Lady is going to be very pleased."

The Lady Juliana was sitting in the church, in her private pew – a large structure with its own roof. She was wearing a bigger head-dress than ever, with two enormous horns, and she had an angry expression on her face. She could hardly admit it, but she was missing the vicar. The good thing about his sermons was that they were totally incomprehensible. All you had to do was to sit and doze while he droned on, or think about what you were having for dinner. In the vicar's absence, however, a new young curate was taking the service. He had a most impertinent manner, which she would have to tell him about afterwards. There he was in the pulpit saying that the rich would find it as hard to get to heaven as a camel going through the eye of a needle – quite unnecessary, and not true either. This sort of thing made people discontented, stopped them paying their rent and made them ask for time off work when they said they were ill.

Suddenly there was a stir. Old Thomas came into the church and everyone turned round to look.

"It's the young lord, m'lady," he whispered. "He's back!'

A glint came into the Lady's eyes. She rose in her seat, to the consternation of the young curate. "Stop the service at once!" she said in a loud voice. "We will hear this sermon at another time." She turned towards the congregation. "Your young lord has returned from a long and difficult pilgrimage. Everyone will go outside and give him three cheers."

There was a scramble as the villagers stood up and pushed to get out. When Will and John rode into the churchyard, there was a crowd of people of all ages standing on both sides of the church door.

Framed in the doorway stood the Lady, huge in her horny head-dress. Her arms were folded upon her bosom.

"Three cheers for the lord!' croaked old Thomas, waving his arms. "Hip, hip, hooray!" they shouted noisily. Thomas put his finger to his lips. There was a sudden silence.

John dismounted from his horse and knelt in front of his mother, in the proper knightly manner. Will stayed in the saddle. He suddenly noticed that his hands were shaking.

"So you have got here at last!" said the Lady. She thought for a moment. "You seem to have been away a remarkably short time. Have you got my rosary and my bottle of Dead Sea water?"

"Madam," said John. He tried to remember what it said about returning from pilgrimages in The Knight's Book of Good Manners. "We salute you, and we offer our prayers for your good health and … and our thanks to God for our safe return."

The Lady towered above him. "What have you been doing?" she asked. "You must have had very swift voyages to come back home so soon."

"Now for it," thought Will. His teeth began to chatter.

John stood up, bowed to his mother, and took a deep breath. "I'm afraid," he said, "we didn't actually get there."

"What!" said the Lady, unfolding her arms and putting her fists on her hips. A murmur went round the crowd. "He says they didn't get there!" People looked at each other with cross and puzzled expressions.

"We were delayed in the mountains," said John, "and we had to use our money for other things. In the end, we couldn't afford to go on and we were too late to reach Jerusalem and get back before winter."

"And where is the vicar?" she demanded.

"He was separated from us," said John. "But we have heard that he set off safely with the rest of the pilgrims. He should be coming back in about two months."

"And what about my Dead Sea water?" said the Lady, her face growing dark.

"I am sorry, madam," said John, "but I will do my best to get it for you at another time."

"Another time!" shouted the Lady angrily. "This time is bad enough. Dallying on the way. Squandering your money. Coming home too soon. Shaming me in front of the whole village! How shall I ever look people in the face again? All this religion! I blame the vicar. You should never have taken him with you." She turned to the trembling Thomas and the rest of her men. "Attend me home, at once."

The Lady swept out, her household servants scurrying after her. She glared at Will as she passed him. The crowd began to talk, in little scandalised conversations. It was clear that the villagers were as angry as the Lady. Will's mother came out from the crowd. "What's to do, Will?" she said. "Where's my present from Jerusalem?"

"The lord has told you," answered Will indignantly. 'We stopped to help some poor people. It cost us a lot of money. Then there was a landslide. So we had to come back."

"You wait till I get you home!" she said threateningly, and shook her stick at him.

"Helping poor people in forrin countries!" said a scowling old man. "What about poor people in this village?"

"Why couldn't he spend his money here," said another, "giving the village a mouthful of meat and a sup of drink?"

"Going all that way and coming back without ever getting there! Now we're shamed before all the other villages," said a third.

"Drat all these lords and ladies, say I," muttered a fourth, not too loudly in case anyone heard him. The crowd broke up and moved out of the churchyard, grumbling as they went.

John and Will were left alone with their horses. "Don't worry, Will," said John. "They don't understand and they'll all forget about it – eventually. Let's go inside." They fastened their reins to a post and entered the church.

The church, as usual, was dim and cold and smelt of damp. They walked up the main aisle to the wooden screen which shut off the eastern part and had a door in the middle. They opened the door, passed through and came up towards the altar. John knelt, and Will got down beside him. "Now we say our thanks," said John, "for our safe return."

They both stayed kneeling for some minutes, silently. After Will had said his prayer, he made the sign of the cross on his chest and said to himself very softly, "From the fury of the Lady Juliana, good Lord deliver us." Then he spoke to John. "Was it all a failure, like they said, master?"

John did not answer for a moment or two. Then he said, "No. We tried to go on pilgrimage and we were diverted to do something else. What we did was right. We can always go on pilgrimage another time. The main thing is that people are alive who might have died. And perhaps we were led there for that purpose."

"It doesn't seem fair," said Will. "You say we did what was right, but we had our money stolen and stones thrown at us. Now we're back here, and everyone's blaming us."

"That happens to people who get involved," said John. "Lots of people don't – but then, they have to live with being uncaring and selfish. I don't want to be like that and I don't think you do. We went to Jerusalem in our hearts, even if we didn't arrive there really."

"Anyway," he added, "I've had an idea. There's a group of knights, the Knights of St John, who do these sorts of things. They run hospitals, and protect pilgrims, and free hostages. They have a headquarters in London, and they go to Greece and other places, and Jerusalem. I'm going to write and ask to see what they do, and help – perhaps for a year. Will you come?"

Will's eyes lit up. "To Greece! I will." He felt half-delivered already.

There is one other curious twist to the story. It happened the following February. John and Will had gone up to London to work with the Knights of St John and the Lady was finishing her dinner in the manor house, when Thomas hobbled in with some excitement. "Now the vicar's back, m'lady," he said.

"Good heavens!" cried the Lady Juliana. "I had given him up for lost." The door opened and the vicar shambled in, very tattered and muddy. "Vicar!" she exclaimed. "Where have you been?"

"Well, I've been all round the world," said the vicar apologetically. "We were blown off our course on the way to Jerusalem, and we went to Spain by mistake. Then we were chased by pirates. We ended up in Greece, and on the way back we lost ourselves in Egypt, or was that on the way there? I can't remember. We seem to have been everywhere."

"Have you got me my Dead Sea water?" enquired the Lady. "I suppose this is the last chance I shall have to ask anybody for it."

"Oh, yes indeed," said the vicar. He delved into a pocket of his cloak and brought out a large bottle, full of murky water. He set it on the table in front of the Lady.

She took a look at it, and frowned. "It's flat and dirty," she said. "Lady Pine's is beautifully clear, and sparkles."

"I assure you, dear Lady," replied the vicar, "it is really from the Dead Sea. That's what the Dead Sea is like. I saw it myself. It's dead; just … dead. Well and truly … dead." His voice trailed away.

"Ah, real Dead Sea water!" commented the Lady. "Lady Pyne's is obviously a fake. I shall tell her so." Her face lightened. "You must be hungry, vicar. Thomas, bring him a plate."

The vicar, who seemed to be famished, sat down and began to eat, describing his journey between the mouthfuls. "Of course, I was so sorry to miss John and Will on the way," he said, "through a silly mistake of my own. But I don't see how they reached Jerusalem in front of us, even though we left them behind."

"They didn't," said Juliana instantly. "They fooled about in the Alps and lost all their money."

"But that's what I don't understand," said the vicar. "I saw them most clearly and distinctly at Jerusalem, in the church where Jesus was buried. I was at the back of the church, and it was crowded. I looked towards the front and I saw Master John standing there, with Will beside him. I could only see the backs of their heads at first, but then they turned to talk to each other, and I saw it was them."

"How can they have been there?" said Juliana impatiently. "You must have been dreaming, vicar."

"No indeed, I insist," expostulated the vicar. "I saw them with these very eyes, three times, three separate days. Then they disappeared. I waited to see them come out, but they didn't. I asked at all the pilgrim inns, and they weren't there. So I thought I'd check. I asked to see the visitors' book in the church. And I looked, and there it was, in his writing: John Speke de Brierleigh. And underneath, Will of the Kitchen."

"They do say that travel broadens the mind," said the Lady icily. "In your case, vicar, it seems to have muddled it up. I hope you will now go straight to your vicarage and send that impertinent young curate packing." She rose from the table and retreated to the parlour, hugging her precious bottle.

The vicar finished his meal and mumbled to himself a good deal. But, for the rest of his life, he insisted that John and Will had really got to Jerusalem.

Chapter 4

THE NEW BOOK

The boy gave a last tug at the bellrope. High overhead, the bell in the church tower clanged again, rang once more faintly, and stopped. Silence followed, so deep that he could hear the beat of his heart in his body. He walked slowly towards the door of the tower, cautiously raised the latch with the lightest of clicks and eased open the door an inch or two. Then he peeped through the gap into the church.

The church was full of people. There was nothing strange about that on a June Sunday morning. But something was wrong. The inside was crowded with men and youths, far more than usually came to services, but there were no women or girls. From the tower door only the backs of the men were visible, but the boy could see that some held staffs in their hands, and others had knives and clubs. He could feel their menace and anger.

The far end of the church – the chancel – was shut off by a wooden screen with a carved and decorated canopy, just as it had been in the time of John and Will. From behind this screen a voice began to speak – a weak, elderly voice, which you could hardly hear from a distance. "Our father, which art in heaven, hallowed be thy name." The voice began to stammer and tremble. "Thy – thy kingdom come. Thy will be done. Be done in earth, as it is in heaven."

The crowd gave a shiver of rage. From near the front, a large man walked forward with a club and beat it on the door to the screen. "We have warned you, priest! We will not have these new prayers. Get out the old book, and give us the Latin service!"

A short pause followed. Then the door of the screen opened and the vicar came out – a tall, frail figure in a shabby white surplice. His face, too, was white. He looked with fear at the crowd. Some of the men had blackened their faces; others wore masks or scarves wrapped round their heads. All carried weapons.

"Bring out the old book!" shouted the large man again. "We will not have words in English, like a children's Christmas play. For three weeks you have said this mockery and we will not allow it any more. We will have the Latin prayers, like we have always had, the prayers that fly up to the saints." The crowd shifted, and murmurs of "Yes, the old book!" filled the church.

The vicar licked his lips. "It – it is the king's will," he said, looking towards the ground. "The new book is commanded by the king and the parliament." Then, gathering his courage together, "I disobey them, if I do not say it. And you disobey them, if you do not hear it quietly."

"It is not the king's will!" yelled the large man. "The king is a child and he is ruled by traitors and false heretics!" The crowd roared its approval. "The new book has changed the old ways. The Cornish have risen against it and the men of Sampford and Dartmoor. The whole land curses it. This is your last chance. Put the new book away, or we will take it from you."

"I must do the will of the king," said the vicar.

"Then we shall do the will of the people! Dick, Hob, Jack – in there, and take it away!"

There was a rush of men towards the screen. Pushing the vicar aside, they ran into the chancel. They seized a large book from the desk in front of the vicar's seat and carried it out. The large man leered in the vicar's face and struck him hard on the chest. The vicar fell backwards, hitting his head on the floor.

"Take that!" cried the ruffian. "Take that for using new words in our church! Now, burn the book!"

"Aye, burn it! Into the fire!" shouted other voices. The crowd turned, jostling through the church door out into the summer sunshine. In a few moments its shouts could be heard in the churchyard.

The boy, who did not understand what had happened, pulled open the tower door and ran to the screen. The sexton appeared from the shadows and they bent over the old man on the floor. He raised his head and groaned.

"Oh master, master!" said the boy.

"I am hurt, but not badly," said the vicar. "Help me up." They raised him to his feet. He tottered, breathing heavily, and rubbed the back of his head. "I had better go to the house. There can be no service here today."

"Go out through the little door," said the sexton urgently. "They may not see us if we go that way." He opened it and they led the vicar out. Smoke from a bonfire blew across the churchyard. The mob was burning the new prayer book and a cheer went up as the book was thrown on the flames. The crowd was far too busy to notice them leaving.

They brought the vicar into his house, helped him upstairs to his chamber and laid him on his bed. He began to breathe more easily. "Take some ale to restore you, master," said the sexton. The boy ran downstairs and came back with a leather tankard. He held it to his master's lips, and the vicar drank. He motioned the tankard away.

"It is all right now. I am not hurt, except for a bruise or two. They have done greater hurts – to God, the king and themselves. That is what saddens me. But it is not surprising, with the news that came this morning."

"The rebels have captured Kirton," said the sexton eagerly, "only seven miles away. Nothing can stop them reaching Ayster. Dick Blackgrease and Jack Upcott heard the news and they roused the men to attack the church. Now, they are going to join the rebels. The city will be cut off by this evening."

The boy listened. "Will they capture the city?" he asked.

The sexton looked scornful. "How can they? Don't you know the saying 'Ayster walls are stronger than the hills'? The Romans built them: three miles long, five great gates and fifteen towers. The city can hold out for months and by then the king's men will come."

The vicar opened his mouth as if to speak. Then he looked at the sexton. "I am better now, Simon," he said. "You can go about your work. Luke will stay with me." When the sexton had clattered down the stairs, the vicar beckoned the boy nearer. "Luke, boy, come closer," he whispered. "There – there is something weighing upon me. All is not well. If the city falls, the king will lose one fifth of his kingdom. Others will rise against him and there will be civil war in the land, as there was in the time of the Roses."

"But surely," said Luke, "surely Ayster will hold out?"

"The mayor and citizens will try," said the vicar. "They do not all love the new book, but none of them wants the Cornish in the city plundering the shops. They think they will be safe inside their walls, but the walls alone will not save them, for all the five great gates and fifteen towers. There is a key to the city that the city does not hold, and it will be the key of the kingdom. You know the old saying about the horseshoe nail?"

"What?" said Luke. "For want of a nail the shoe was lost. For want of a shoe the horse was lost. For want of a horse the rider was lost."

"Exactly so," said the vicar. "And you could go on. For want of a rider the battle was lost. For want of a battle the kingdom was lost. And all for the want of a horseshoe nail."

"But what do you mean?" asked Luke.

"I mean," said the vicar, "that the safety of the king and the throne depends on something as small as a horseshoe nail. Water. Ayster's water comes from outside the city. It rises in a spring, and is led inside the walls through underground passages. The rebels know this and they will look for the spring. When they find it, they will dig trenches and divert it. The city has some wells, but in the middle of summer they can never supply everyone. And thirst weakens people far sooner than hunger."

"Then," said Luke with alarm, "the city is doomed, and the king."

"That is what troubles me," said the vicar, "because it need not happen. There is water in the city, if people knew where it was. Let me tell you this story. When I lived in the city, there was a Frenchman there, called Master Guiscard. He was a merchant, but the other merchants despised him for being a foreigner. I can speak French and we often spoke it together. He would invite me to his house and entertain me. One year, there was a great drought and the city's springs ran low. Master Guiscard thought he would dig a hole in his cellar to make a well, but when he dug he found a cave with water running through it.

It was not the same as the city water, because it ran strongly in spite of the drought, but afterwards he always drew his water from it. I have seen it myself. There is enough water there to save the city. But Master Guiscard is long dead and Madam Guiscard lived alone in the house many years, seeing no one. She has just died and I doubt if the cave is known to anyone. If the spring could be found, the city would be safe."

Luke said, "How can we tell the city?"

"That is the problem," answered the vicar. "Until yesterday I never thought that rebels would ever come to the city again. This morning at dawn, I decided to ride into Ayster at once, but the men of the village are guarding the roads. They are afraid the rebels will take their cattle and they are letting no one in or out. They stopped me and sent me back."

Luke thought. "Could I go?" he asked.

"There is a chance," said the vicar. "They might let you past, or you might slip by and get into the city before the rebels arrive. Will you try?"

It was a challenge. Luke said at once, "I will."

"Then go now. Put on old clothes, and carry some food in case you need it. Go along fast before the rebels come."

"Whom must I tell?" asked Luke.

"You must find the mayor," said the vicar. "Or one of the council. I will not give you anything in writing in case it is found. Remember the message by heart. This is the way. First, go to the High Street, then to Rose Lane. Thirdly, go to the seventh house on the right, and lastly, go to the cellar. If necessary, you will have to stay in the city. In that case, look for Master Hooker. He is a young man who writes letters for the mayor and he is for the new book. He will look after you. I will tell your family where you are."

Five minutes later, Luke was in his attic room taking off his cassock and putting on his oldest, raggedest clothes. He went downstairs, took bread, meat and a leather bottle of ale from the kitchen and put them into a bag which he hoisted on to his back. Then he raced out into the lane by the church, full of excitement about his mission. His first thought was to ask his friends to come. The Green Men they called themselves, and they had often played at wars and secret missions in the woods. Now they could do it for real. But there was no one in the church lane. The bonfire in the churchyard was still smoking, but the crowd had gone.

He walked up and down the high street, hoping to see his friends. The only person about was a girl, standing outside a tumbledown cottage. She wore a grubby dress and had bare feet. Luke knew her well by sight. She was one of a large, poor family, whose children ran wild about the village. Sible her name was; she would sometimes come to the vicarage door for bread or scraps. This morning, he disdained to notice her. But she spoke to him, all the same.

"Looking for Will and Drew?" she asked.

"Yes," he said shortly.

"They've gone to see the rebels."

Bother. He would have to ask her for help. "Which way?"

"Up Berry Hill."

"Thanks," he said reluctantly. He started to walk off.

She spoke again. "They left a message for you."

This astounded him. The Green Men were all boys and they despised the girls of the village. "What is it?" he said.

"They said … " She stopped, apparently trying to tone down a message. "They said they're on a different side from you. They are for the old book, you are for the new one."

"What does that mean?"

"They don't want you. That's what they said. They told me to tell you."

He felt stunned, as if by a blow. He wasn't on the side of the new book. He was just the vicar's servant, doing jobs in return for learning to read. His parents wanted him to become a priest. It wasn't fair – his friends had cast him off without a chance to defend himself. And they had sent their message through a girl – the worst possible insult. Tears came into his eyes.

The girl looked at him. She said, "Let's go and watch the rebels too. We can go a different way."

"I can't," he answered, blinking back his tears. "I've got a message to take." He wondered what to do. If the Green Men had gone up Berry Hill, he would cross the fields and go to Ayster by another road. He walked away, but before he had gone a few yards he realised she was following.

She said, "Let's go through the fields, and see the rebels by the bridge." This was exactly the way he was planning to go. He jerked his bag on his shoulder, angrily.

"I don't want company," he said. "I want to go by myself."

She seemed to take no notice. "I'm not a rebel, either," she said. He quickened his pace; she quickened hers, with determination. After a bit, she added, "I agree with the new book." This annoyed him more. What right did she have to an opinion about it? He kept his mouth tightly shut.

"The rebels say they want the old book. But they never came to church when they had it, did they?" she said. "I've seen them in the pub on Sunday mornings. They say they're the ones who are right. Well, if they're right, why did they hit the vicar?"

Luke felt surprised. He had never really thought about the new book. He did what the vicar told him, because he was the vicar's servant. The quarrels about the book had been rather a joke, until the men came to church with their faces black. But still he said nothing. Presently, they reached a lane and drew near to the high road leading to Ayster. It became clear that they could go no further. A cart was wedged across the lane and a group of men stood around it. Smoke rose from a campfire. These were men from the village on guard.

"And where are you going, young Luke?" said the nearest man. "No way for you. The people are marching past, against the new book." In the distance, on the high road, there was a stream of men on foot, on horses and in carts. "Go home – and you, Sible. This is no place for children."

Luke felt a second shock of disappointment. He wondered whether to say he was taking a message. But no; they would be suspicious, and in any case, it was too late. The rebels were already nearing the city. He could not walk along the roads without being seen and questioned – perhaps even being made to join them. He turned round. The girl did the same. They walked back down the lane, back across the fields,

"Where are you taking your message?" she asked.

He felt downcast. He would have to go back to the vicar and say he had failed. "It doesn't matter," he answered. "I'll do it later."

They walked a little further. Then she said, "If you want to see the rebels, we can go to another place."

Luke wanted only to escape from her, but he could not resist asking. "Where?"

"We can cross the river to Woodstoke, by the footbridge." Woodstoke was the next village westwards.

Luke thought it was worth trying. There was a chance of leaving Brierleigh on the west side, and reaching Ayster from a different direction. But he said nothing until they were back in the village. When they reached her house, he said, "Goodbye. I'm going home."

"Aren't you coming to Woodstoke?" she asked.

"No." He left her and went into the vicarage garden. Looking round to make sure she had gone, he scrambled through a hole in the hedge, came into a field and made his way along the edge of the river towards the footbridge. He climbed on to the bridge and gave a sigh. There was another picket of men at the end of the bridge. The Brierleigh men were taking good care to guard their village and their cattle.

He stood by the end of the bridge for a little until he heard footsteps approaching. To his annoyance, Sible appeared again. She had come round by the road. "You said you were going home," she said.

"Well, I didn't go," he answered crossly.

"They won't let us out this way, either," she observed, seeing the picket in the distance. "All the same, anyone could go out if they wanted."

"How?"

"I'll tell you if you'll let me come with you," she said.

"I can't," he answered. "I'm going by myself. It's too dangerous for a girl."

"Where are you going then?" she said.

Luke considered. He didn't want her company, but he needed help. "Let's go somewhere else," he said. "Then we can talk about it."

They left the bridge, walked through a gate and sat under a tree. "Tell me how to get out," he said.

"Cross your heart you'll let me come," she challenged him.

"All right," he said reluctantly.

"Do it then."

Very slowly, he made the sign of the cross on his chest. "I promise."

"Where do you want to go?" she asked.

"I've got to take a message," he said, "to a house down the river." He did not want to say Ayster.

"Well," she said, "you could go in a boat. I know where there is one. If you went at night, no one would see you."

"Where is it?"

"I'll show you when the time comes," she said teasingly. "When shall we go?"

"It gets dark at about nine," he said.

She stood up, as if the matter was settled. "All right. I'll meet you here."

"Will your parents let you?" he asked, hoping that this might cause a problem.

"They'll think I'm in bed," she answered scornfully. "But I'll be here." Her eyes were bright. "It's an adventure. Goodbye." She ran lightly away and disappeared.

Luke stayed sitting in the field. Thoughts crowded in. Leaving the village by boat was a solution. The river ran past the city of Ayster and you could drift along it in the dark without anyone being the wiser. A way had been opened for him, but Sible had found it and he would have to take her with him. He pondered what to do. He wouldn't go back to the vicarage in case he met the Green Men or the vicar. It was mid afternoon. Better to stay here hidden until night fall. He had food with him, and his bottle of ale.

He sat on, thinking. Why was he going? Because the vicar had asked him. But why was that right? His friends would call him a traitor. Unwillingly, he had to agree with Sible. It was true. The men of the village had never bothered about the church until now. They had claimed to be doing right and then they had attacked the vicar. His friends had deserted him too – for the old book. If the old book made people like that, perhaps having a new one would be better. He felt it was important to sort that out, to know that what he was doing was worth it. When he had decided that it was, he relaxed and began to feel drowsy. The day was warm and close. He fell asleep for a long time. When he woke up, he had some food and heard the church clock strike six. He passed the remaining three hours with increasing impatience. At last it began to grow dark. Nine o'clock struck. Where was she?

Presently, he heard a rustling across the grass and she came. She had changed into a dark-brown dress, and she wore an old pair of shoes. "It's over there," she said. He followed her through the field and into another, fringed with clumps of reeds. She led him to the biggest patch of reeds, parted their stems and showed him a wooden punt, containing two paddles.

He knew it at once. "It's Farmer Sowden's," he said.

"Yes," she said. "He hid it here because of the rebels. I watched him."

Luke decided he had better try to stop her from coming. "Sible," he said. "If I tell you something, will you keep it secret?"

She crossed herself. "Promise."

"I have to take a message into Ayster. But the rebels are outside it now. I don't think you should come."

She answered instantly. "Well, then, you can't go either. You can't paddle the punt on your own – you need two people."

"But if we get there, we may not be able to come back."

"We'll find a way," she said lightly.

"What about your parents?"

"They'll think I've gone to my gran's. Anyway, we have a cousin in the city."

This ended his last chance of going alone. Together, they pushed the boat into the water. Together, they got in – she in the front, he in the back, with a paddle on each side. Together, they glided down the river. It was not hard to paddle, because they were going downstream. Although the river twisted and turned, the night was clear and there was enough starlight to show where the banks lay.

After some time they approached the Long Bridge. Voices in the distance told them that people were standing on it. Every now and again lights could be seen moving across. The last rebels were still making their way towards Ayster and it was possible that they had set a watch on the bridge.

"We had better wait," Luke said to Sible. "Let's go into the bank."

They steered towards a thicket of bushes by the riverside and stopped. They stayed there for some time. Gradually, as midnight approached, the movements on the bridge grew fewer and then stopped altogether.

"Let's go on," he whispered.

"All right," she answered. "Don't splash with the paddle. Go quietly."

They drifted with the current towards the bridge and went through the central arch. Luke felt that his luck was turning at last. There were men up above, talking together, but nobody noticed the punt go by in the water. When it was well away from the bridge, they started to paddle again.

Gradually, the river grew wider. They could see the outline of a hill on their left. Soon the outline was broken by roofs and towers. They were approaching Ayster. Luke called softly to Sible, "We shall have to be careful now. There is another bridge. We ought to land on the left bank before we get to it, where the town comes down to the water. We can tie up somewhere."

In the end, they managed very well. By the edge of the city, they found a small pier jutting out over the river on pillars. A ladder came down into the water. They steered the punt under the pier, and tied it up near the ladder.

"I wonder what time it is," said Luke.

"A clock struck three just now," said Sible. "What shall we do next?"

"I think we ought to climb up on to the land while it's still dark," he answered. "Then we'll hide until morning." So they scaled the ladder, walked along the pier, and into a lane with overhanging houses.

"There are bound to be soldiers about," said Luke. "Let's go and ask if we can see the mayor."

No sooner had he spoken than there was a shout.

"Spies! Treason!" A lantern flashed in front of him and his arm was caught and held. "Spies here, Jem and Richard! Pikes to the ready!" A group of men rushed out of a nearby alley, their weapons glinting in the light of the lantern. Sible dodged and fled along the lane. There was a noise of heavy boots as two men pounded after her.

"Who are you?" said a rough voice. The lantern was pushed towards Luke's face. "Why, it's a boy," said another voice.

"Where's the man who was with you?" The grip on Luke's arm tightened, and he was shaken.

"There isn't a man," he said. He felt betrayed again. Sible had fled. But he said firmly, "I'm on my own."

"Liar! There was a man with you. Two of my men are chasing him. Come here." Luke was dragged away.

"We've found a spy," said the leader. "Maybe two. Bring in this one. Richard and Jem have gone for the other." Luke was hustled through a gateway into a vaulted room with lights burning. Soon, the two men who had chased Sible came back. She was not with them.

"Escaped!" they said. "We'll have a good search when it gets light."

"Escaped?" said the leader. He turned to Luke. "Now, who are you, and who were you with?"

"I want to see the mayor," said Luke. "I've brought a message for him."

"You'll see the mayor all right," said the leader. "You little spy! Where's the man who brought you?"

"There wasn't a man," said Luke.

The leader scowled at Luke. "We'll find him. You can go to the gaol in the Guildhall. The mayor will examine you later. We hang spies here!" he hissed.

Luke's arms were tied behind his back and a rope was put round his neck. He was then led by two men up the empty High Street to the Guildhall. There, he was handed over to a gaoler, untied and thrown into a small, dark, empty room with no furniture. The door was locked behind him.

Luke sat on the floor. He felt hungry, but his bag had been taken away. Gradually, the grey light of morning came in through the small cell window. It was the second time that he had been betrayed. First, his old friends, now the new one. Sible had forced her company on him, and then she had left him. Why? Had she just got scared and run away? Well, now he was on his own without any girls, as he had always wanted. Somebody would come soon and take him to the mayor. He would be able to give his message, by himself. But nothing happened. An hour passed, and another. Noises began in a street outside, the noises of everyday life. More time went by; it seemed to be the middle of the morning.

Suddenly, there were approaching footsteps. He stood up. At last they were coming.

The door was opened. To his amazement, Sible came in. "They've caught you!" he said.

"No," she answered, her eyes shining. "I hid. Then I came in through the gate. Then I found this gentleman, Master Hooker, and he is taking us to see the mayor." Standing behind her was a young man dressed in black with a kind face. He came into the cell.

"Are you the boy from Brierleigh?" he asked. "Why have you come to the city?"

"I have a message, sir," said Luke. "It is from our vicar, Master Harris, for the mayor. It is to save the city from the rebels." He proceeded to tell the vicar's message.

"You have both done well to bring this news," said the young man. "It could be important. I think I will take you to see the mayor now. He is very busy and I warn you, he is a hasty man, with a lot of trouble today. The rebels are all round the city and he has to organise the defence. But come outside, and we will see what we can do."

They followed him out of the cell; up steps, and along a

passage into a great beamed hall. The mayor was sitting on a kind of throne, talking to several people below him. He was a large man with close-cropped hair and an angry expression. He was wearing a red robe. The young man brought Luke and Sible forward and waited for the mayor's attention.

Eventually, the mayor looked up. The young man bowed and explained who they were. Luke was made to tell his story again.

"Who told you this?" snapped the mayor, interrupting. "Master Harris? Never heard of him! It's nonsense anyway. The water all comes in by underground passages. The springs are far too deep for the rebels to find. The water is the one thing we can be quite sure about."

"Even so, sir," said the young man, "shouldn't we tell the people to start storing water, in case anything happens?"

"All right then. Have it proclaimed round the city," said the mayor shortly. "I'm off to the walls. I'll be back in an hour." He came down from his seat and took off his robe. He was wearing armour underneath. He stamped out of the hall, with his men behind him.

"I must get the town crier to tell people to store water," said the young man. "But meanwhile, I expect you'd like some breakfast. There isn't much food, but we can probably find you some rations."

He left them in a kitchen where they were given bread and cheese and ale. Luke ate his without speaking. Sible looked at him. "I didn't want to leave you," she said. "I was scared when those soldiers came. That's why I ran. But I followed you."

"I know," said Luke. Why had he doubted her? She had been faithful to him. It was just so hard to accept her as equal, to hear her being praised for coming as well as himself. But, he had to admit, he could not have come so far without her. And she had stood up with him for the new book. He looked at her and gave a small smile. "Thanks," he said.

They stayed in the kitchen until the young man came back. "Let's go out and see about this house of yours." They went out of the Guildhall into the High Street, straight into the end of a long queue of woman with buckets. The queue went down the street to a fountain, which stood at the crossroads in the middle of the city. The fountain consisted of a stone pillar with a lion's head on it. Water poured out of the lion's mouth into a basin, and you filled a bucket by placing it under the mouth.

The mayor had returned. He seized a bucket from an onlooker.

"Right, everyone!" he bellowed. "Hold your bucket under the stream. Fill it nearly to the top. Like this. Then move on quickly, for the next man." He held the bucket under the stream to demonstrate. As he did so, the stream of water faltered. It pulsed twice and died away to a trickle, then to a drip. The mayor looked shaken.

"Something's happened to the water!" he announced unnecessarily. "People must be drawing it off, somewhere else. Go to the other fountain and see." Three of his men ran down the street.

The young man went up to the mayor. "Perhaps, sir, it would be a good idea if I took these messengers to the house they talk of, to see if there is any water there."

"Well, get on with it!" shouted the mayor. "We can't have people queuing here for nothing." There was a cry in the distance. "The other fountain has gone dry as well."

The bucket-carriers surged round the mayor, arguing and

complaining. "Come on," said the young man, pushing his way through the crowd. Luke and Sible followed him. When they were clear of the people, the young man said, "Now, where was this house you spoke of?"

"In Rose Lane, off the High Street," said Luke.

"That's this way," said the young man pointing ahead. They walked along the street for some distance and turned into a narrow cobbled lane with a drain in the middle and houses jutting out over it. They went round a corner. "We have to find the seventh house on the right," said Luke.

The seventh house did not face directly into the lane but into a yard at the side, approached through a wall with a gateway in it. They pushed at the door in the gateway, which was stiff but not locked, and shoved it open. Inside, was a yard in front of an ancient house. Weeds grew up between the flagstones. The door of the house was locked.

"I'll go next door and see if they have the key," said the young man. After a short time, he returned with a neighbour and the key and opened the door.

The house had a curious feeling about it. The hall lay still and peaceful. There were a polished oak table, chairs and fire-irons, all of the best quality and tidily arranged except for a thin layer of dust. In the chamber next door was a four-poster bed, with curtains and coverings of fine cloth decorated with roses. There was a faint fragrance coming from bowls of dried herbs on the window sills. Sible went to one of these and stirred the contents with her fingers. Houses tell you what has happened in them. This one said, "Those who lived here were polite and kind. Everything was of the finest, everything was well ordered, everything was peaceful. There were no quarrels, no disorders. And this house will never forget."

Behind the hall was a passage leading to a strong oak door. The two men heaved it open. A flight of steps went down to the cellar which smelt strongly of wine. Here, there was a trapdoor in the floor which was easily raised by a large iron ring. They opened it and were greeted by the sound of water – a strong, deep stream, running along underneath.

An hour later, the mayor had made his appearance and was organising a new bucket chain through the yard into the lane. The queue of bucket-holders had gathered again. The young man led the children away and back to the High Street.

"You have certainly saved the city," he said, "and not only the city – the new book. When the mayor is not so busy, he will be grateful. After the siege is over, the city too will show its gratitude. It will offer you money or something else that you want."

"I don't need anything," said Luke. "I am apprenticed to a priest." He looked at Sible and paused. Then he added, "Sible might."

"I would like to live in a house like that," said Sible, "and sell things in a market."

"We can arrange that," said the young man. "We can make you an apprentice to learn a trade. Then you will live in a house in the city and go to market."

He asked them what they wished to do next. "The old book cannot win now but the rebels may besiege the city for weeks. Do you want to stay here?"

"I wish I could go back to Brierleigh," said Luke. "Master Harris will worry about his message and I would like to tell him what has happened. But how would we get out?"

"That may not be as hard as coming in," said the young man.

"This afternoon, a cart is going out to Twyford, down the Woodstoke road. It is carrying a nobleman's goods and we think that the rebels will let it through. We can hide you among the bags and the driver will drop you in the countryside. If you are careful, you may reach home without anyone knowing where you have been."

Nothing seemed too hard for him to solve. He even promised to find the punt and look after it. He took them to the cart and introduced them to the drivers. He said goodbye and saw them placed in the middle of the luggage, with bags and boxes around them. Presently, they felt the cart jolting along the streets. There was a sound of the drawing back of bolts and doors and it passed out of the city gate. They could hear the noise of the rebels outside and the carters shouting that they were the earl's men and had safe-conduct. Nobody interfered with them. They jogged and rattled along for nearly an hour, and were put down by the roadside, a couple of miles north of their village.

They came back over the fields, looking out cautiously for pickets. But there was no one on this side of the village. Luke felt glad with success. "We got there," he said. "The new book has been saved." Then he made an effort and added, "I couldn't have done it without you."

Sible looked at him and suddenly kissed him on the mouth. He blushed and looked away. Then he took her hand. A little way further on, they kissed each other.

"If I go into Ayster to be an apprentice," she said, "will you come and see me?"

"Yes," he answered.

The siege of the city lasted for four weeks, until the king's men drove the rebels away. The day after the siege was over, a deputation of the village men shuffled through the vicarage door to make their peace with the vicar. The city offered Luke a church if he became a priest, but Sible went to be an apprentice that very autumn. It was a pure coincidence that her master and mistress bought the house in Rose Lane.

Chapter 5

SECRET TREASURE

One August afternoon in 1710, when Queen Anne was on the throne, the carrier's cart stopped by a farmhouse gate in Brierleigh. The carrier jumped from his seat, lifted down a box and said to the girl who was sitting beside him, "Here's 'Paradise', Miss."

The girl, called Verity, was coming to stay at the farm with her mother's aunt, Miss Westaway. "I don't suppose you'll want to go," said her mother when the invitation came. "Aunt Esther is very kind, to be sure, but she's old-fashioned and odd in her ways, with her manservant and her morbidge* and her secret treasure – it's a strange place to stay."

Verity had no such doubts. Holidays were rare events for her and two or three weeks in an old house sounded exciting. Even the name of it, "Paradise", was enticing. "Is there really a treasure?" she asked.

"It's a story in the family," said her mother. "Bags and bags of gold, hidden somewhere in the house. Many's the time I looked when I was young. But the place has so many cupboards and cellars and old thick walls that no one has ever been able to find it." Verity at once decided that she would do so. She would go round the house very carefully, poking into corners and tapping the walls, until she discovered the gold. How pleased her aunt would be!

Now though, as she climbed down from the cart, she felt shy and a little alarmed. A sound of shrill, excited barking could be heard from inside the farmhouse door, followed by a deeper

* Everyone in the story calls it this, but the real word is mortgage. Aunt Esther explains what it is on page 108.

bark in the distance: rougher and more menacing.

"Is it safe to go in?" she asked doubtfully.

"Bless you," said the carrier, "he's nothing but a puppy. It's the one down the road you've got to watch." He walked up to the farmhouse door, put down the box, knocked loudly and went back to the cart.

At that moment the door opened a little and out rushed a small spaniel dog of the kind that King Charles II was fond of. He ran straight to Verity, raced round her several times and jumped at her waist, barking continuously. Meanwhile the door opened wider and out stepped a dame with white hair, spectacles on her nose and a white apron over a dress that swished and rustled as she came. This was Aunt Esther.

"He's gone," said the dame. "I wanted to catch him. Get down, Samuel! Come in, dear. I'm so glad to see you. Samuel! Come here!" In a single movement she managed to kiss Verity, grab the dog by the collar and make a half-turn back towards the door, crying "Jack!"

Out of the doorway came a little man, also dressed in an apron. The dame, still holding Samuel in one hand, flourished the other first at Verity, then at the box, and finally in a vaguely upward direction, saying very loudly, "my niece", "box", and "cock-loft". The small man grinned, bowed, picked up the box and took it inside the house. "He can't hear you, dear, so it's no use shouting at him," said the dame. "He'll take your things up. Come in and have a wash and some tea. Samuel!" she cried to the spaniel, who was emitting a chocking cough from his tightly held collar. "Behave yourself." She released the collar. "Go in, dear," said Aunt Esther. "It's nice to see you."

The front door of the house led into a passage and the

passage into a surprising room, like the great hall of a stately home, but smaller. It had a high sloping roof of rafters, four tall windows and a large empty fireplace. Over the fireplace was a complicated carving, painted white. "Plaster," said Aunt Esther. It showed Adam and Eve with bare bodies and long hair, standing in front of a tree with a serpent coiled round the trunk like a helter-skelter. Eve was holding an apple – "a Devon codling that is," said the dame. "Same as we have in the orchard." On one side was a smaller figure of Adam lying asleep and God drawing Eve from his side, rather like (thought Verity) a magician pulling a rabbit out of a hat. On the other side were Adam and Eve looking glum, being turned out of Paradise by an angel with wings and a sword. This time they were wearing shorts which looked like leaves sewn together.

"What are they wearing?" asked Verity.

"Breeches," said her aunt. "It doesn't say so in our Bible, but it did in an old one of Father's."

The hall led into a smaller room with a flat ceiling, called the parlour. This was a pleasant place. There were comfortable wooden chairs, a table, a bookcase, a chest of drawers and a sideboard full of blue and white china plates. A cord hung from a small wheel on one wall, which the dame pulled with a jerk, and a bell jangled in the depths of the house.

"That'll fetch in Jack," said the dame. Verity wondered how – if he couldn't hear it – but presently the little man came in with a large tray. Again he gave a grin, bowed, set down the tray on the table and withdrew. Aunt Esther sketched a curious kind of curtsy as he went out. "That's how I say 'thank you'," she said.

"Can't he hear at all?" asked Verity.

"Nor speak neither," said her aunt. "Hoeing he used to do, on the land; they wouldn't let him plough or lead the horses. I took him and taught him to cook. He cooks better than me when he's in the mood, and does the other work. He likes it if you thank him, dear. And I'll teach you the signs he knows." She began to unload the tray.

The tea was very good. There were buns, cream and raspberry jam in dishes, a teapot and a milk jug, both of silver.

"Tell me about the treasure, Aunt Esther," said Verity after tea.

"Bags and bags of gold, dear," said her aunt, "sovereigns and marks and angels – all in this house, if only I could find it."

"Where did it come from?"

"It came from the Ancient Days," said the aunt, with a mysterious wave of her hand. "My father was always talking about it when I was a little girl. 'Esther', he'd say to me, 'this house is full of treasure', and then he'd go off into fits of laughter. He was such a joker."

"But didn't he say where it was?"

"He didn't know himself, though he often looked for it. He needed money, for he fought for King Charles and lost his horse and all his things and was poor ever afterwards. He just knew it was here. 'The treasure is here', that's what he'd say, 'and some day you'll know it'.

"So he struggled on with the farm. Then he wanted money badly and he had to borrow some. He got one of those things called a morbidge, and a pity he did, for that has been a trouble ever since."

"What's a morbidge?"

"He borrowed two hundred pounds of gold from a lawyer in

the city. Every year he had to pay back ten pounds to the lawyer. When I was young I thought he was paying back the money. But the ten pounds didn't pay it back at all – that was what they call the interest on the morbidge. And I still have to pay it every year. If I can't pay the ten pounds every year, I shall have to give up the farm. And at the end of a certain time, either the two hundred pounds have to be paid back, or I lose the farm as well."

"Oh," said Verity. She felt embarrassed at being told her aunt's worries. She said, "When is the end of the certain time?"

This time her aunt looked embarrassed. "My father borrowed the money fifty years ago and it had to be paid back in ninety years. That's all right for me, because I can afford ten pounds each year and I shan't be here in forty years' time. But I don't have the paper that says so, though I should have. Mr Standish, my lawyer, says that could be awkward. The man who owns the morbidge might say that the time was up and I couldn't prove that it wasn't."

"Who is the man that owns the morbidge?" asked Verity.

"Oby Blagdon. He's my very own next-door neighbour. His is the farm on the other side – Starveall Farm they call it, because it's poor, sour land. And a hard man he is. He married a rich farmer's daughter and he made money – I won't say how – and he prospered, and bought more land and beasts and hired more men and now he's rich. He wants my house because it's better than his and twice he's offered me pounds of gold to sell it, but I won't. In the end he bought the morbidge from the lawyer to get me into his power, so now I have to pay him the ten pounds a year. If I can't pay, then Paradise Farm, and all my goods will be his and he can search for the treasure. And he'll look well for it and find it.

"Sometimes I think about all this at night and what I should do. But this is a pleasant house and it takes my fears away. Jack and I live well. I have three cows and a few sheep, and Tom comes in to help us keep them. We grow food in our kitchen garden and there are ducks and hens. We have enough to live on and some to give away. But if I could find the treasure, I could pay off the morbidge and then I would be happy. So you must help me look for it while you're here.

"And now, dear," said her aunt, "I'll show you round Paradise." She got up from her chair, tripped over Samuel and pulled open the topmost drawer of the chest of drawers. Verity rose too and saw that the drawer was full of keys. Large keys and small keys, chubby keys and thin keys, brass keys and iron keys, keys with finely decorated handles and keys with intricate curving wards, keys on their own and bunches of keys, and keys with labels covered with faded writing.

"These are the keys!" said Aunt Esther triumphantly. "My father collected them. 'Always look after the drawer with the keys', he used to tell me. I keep the store-cupboard key in it. It's a brass one in a bunch of five. You look for me, dear, I can't see in these spectacles." Verity had a good hunt through. "There are five here with a brass one," she said, trying to read the label, "but I think it says 'kitchen'."

Aunt Esther grabbed the bunch, with a cackle of laughter. "That's the one, dear. Most of the labels are wrong, but it's easy to pick out the right key when you want to."

Verity thought she could understand how the treasure was lost, not to mention the morbidge.

Her aunt led the way out of the parlour and through the hall. On the other side of the hall was the kitchen – a high, whitewashed room with well-scrubbed wooden tables and shelves crowded with shining copper pans of every shape and size. There was an open fireplace with a log fire glowing in it, and hooks hanging down for pots. Jack stood at a table, cutting meat with a cleaver; he grinned, but did not speak. The kitchen led into the scullery, with a pump, a sink and more shelves and pans, and the scullery into the still room ("for herbs and recipes," said Aunt Esther), with sweet-smelling bunches of lavender and rosemary hung up to dry and shelves holding bottles of clear and coloured liquids: saffron yellow, ruby red and pale green. This room had an outside door – like most doors in the house it stuck and gave way suddenly when Esther pushed at it. They tumbled into the open air.

A cobbled path led to a wall and a gate, with a glimpse of many colours inside it. Here there was a beautiful garden of roses. It was completely surrounded by red mud walls topped with tiles and lay warm and still in the late afternoon sunlight. Paths led round it in a square, and to a sundial in the middle. On either side of the paths stood dozens of rose bushes bearing hundreds of blooms – dark red, crimson, pink, yellow, cream and purest white. On the south side of a garden was a substantial stone seat where you could sit and look at the flowers. "Coming on well, they are," said Aunt Esther.

There was another way out of the rose garden. This led to a wide lawn with a long border of tall cottage flowers, several small trees and a pond, edged with flagstones and full of lilies. Two ducks were swimming there. One side of the house looked on this lawn, with a thatched roof and a little window peeping out of it.

"That's the cock-loft," said the dame. "You'll sleep up there."

Verity was quite confused by now. A cock-loft! It sounded like a henhouse; could it be that her aunt kept fowls up in the attic? Anything seemed possible in this strange house. They went in again by the front door and up the stairs. "That's my room," said Aunt Esther, "and yours is here." She opened what looked like a cupboard door and motioned Verity in. Behind the door was a tiny wooden staircase. "Go up, dear," said her aunt. Verity felt her way up, with her aunt rustling behind and Samuel's claws clicking on the bare stairboards, until they came out into a long attic room with sloping ceilings. Inside were a bed with a patchwork quilt of bright colours, a rag rug on the floor, also of many hues, a chest of drawers with a pewter candlestick on the top, a wash-stand and a cupboard ("for putting your clothes in"). The windows were open and a smell of herbs and flowers came in from the garden. The box, brought up by Jack, was on the floor.

"I'll leave you to unpack, dear" said Aunt Esther, "while I find Jack his stores. Come down when you like, and go wherever you like. Supper's at six, and Jack will ring the bell."

The days that followed passed very pleasantly. Verity spent much of the time exploring. She sat on the seat in the rose garden or talked to the ducks (there was a larger pond, full of them, beyond the garden). She watched Tom the cowman milk the cows in the shed. He too, it seemed, could not do real work, being slow and stiff in his legs. If she got bored outside, she could go into the parlour and read the books, of which there were lots. Some of these were difficult books like The Pilgrim's Progress and Mr William Shakespeare's Comedies, Histories and Tragedies, but others were little chap-books of the kind that pedlars sell for a penny or two like Sir Guy of Warwick, Robin Hood and Maid Marian, and The Friar and the Boy – stories of knights and outlaws and magical gifts, with rough little pictures. She went into the kitchen and helped Jack with the food. And she searched for the treasure: opening cupboards and tapping walls. But she found no clue to where it was.

Always, after an hour or two, she heard the jingling of her Aunt Esther's keys or her aunt's high voice calling, and she ran (with Samuel going in and out of her legs) to pick rose petals or herbs, open chests of linen and hang out the pieces to air, polish silver spoons, stir up recipes, or take a plate of food to the old women in the nearby cottages. And there were meals – always excellent ones. Breakfast by herself in the great hall. Midday dinner there with everyone. Supper in the parlour ("it's more comfy there, dear"), while Jack and Tom supped by themselves in the kitchen.

The drawerful of keys, as Verity soon discovered, had nothing to do with "Paradise" as it was run nowadays. Nothing in the house was locked, except for the store-cupboard, and you could wander everywhere – or nearly everywhere. There was just one door that did not open. It was a stout wooden door between two outbuildings, and Verity was curious to see where it led. She pushed at it hopefully, and turned the handle, but the door held fast in the middle, not at the top or bottom. It was certainly locked. She asked her aunt, while they were pounding herbs with pestles.

"Where does the door lead by the barn, the one that is locked?"

"Oh, just to the logs," said her aunt, absent-mindedly. "Make sure you grind it down as small as you can," and the conversation changed. It seemed difficult to mention the matter again. But each day, as she passed the door, Verity thought about it – she even invented a name for it: "The Forbidden Door". It bothered her. She was the treasure seeker, and she felt that she had a right to look behind it. Once she had convinced herself of that, it was not very hard to do so. She had only to go into the parlour when her aunt was elsewhere and look at the keys in the drawer to find the right one. Having inspected the keyhole, she knew it would be a large key, and knowing her aunt's methods of operating, it would not have the proper name on it. She took and tried a key called "cellar" and another marked "front gate", but neither worked. A third, however, labelled "hall", fitted snugly and turned without difficulty.

She waited until dinner was over, when Tom went off to the sheep, and Esther and Jack had a snooze for half an hour. When all was quiet, Verity stole out of the house with the key in her pocket and walked towards the Forbidden Door. She looked to left and right, saw nobody, and fitted the key in the lock. She turned it, opened the door and closed it after her.

She was in a small yard with buildings on two sides: a shabby place with moss growing over the stones. As Aunt Esther had said, there was a pile of logs against the further wall, many of them damp and mouldy. But what gave Verity a shock was a boy, of about her own age, sitting on the tiles on the top of the wall with his knees drawn up. He was wearing a waistcoat over his shirt, knee breeches, stockings and shoes. The boy saw her at once.

"'Oo are you?" he said, twitching a straw in his mouth as he spoke.

"I live here," said Verity. "At least, I'm staying here for a holiday." She paused and added, "on the farm".

"Farm! said the boy scornfully. "Three stringy cows and a sheep. We got a proper farm: forty cattle, and sheep and pigs. We got six men and maids; she've only got Dumb Jack and Bandy Tom. "

"This must be a boy from the farm next door," thought Verity. "Oby Blagdon's farm. Perhaps it's Oby's son." She had no idea what the Blagdon family was like. She looked at the boy; his face was fat and his expression dull and cunning at the same time.

"Is your farm over the wall?" she said.

"Starveall Farm," he replied. "If you was a boy you could see. Girls can't climb."

"I can," said Verity hotly. Actually, it was not difficult to scale the pile of logs and pull herself on to the wall. She sat down, a foot or two away from the boy's shoes.

The view from the top of the wall was not very interesting. On Aunt Esther's side, you could see only the outlying roofs. "Paradise" itself was hidden. On the other side stood Starveall Farm, part mud-built and part brick. It had a sour, gloomy look for a summer's day. The buildings were in bad repair; roofs sagged, windows were boarded up. In the distance, three ragged men were straining to pull a waggon.

"See?" said the boy, through his straw. "We're rich. My dad's going to take over "Paradise" any day now, he says. Then he'll turn her out."

"He can't," said Verity indignantly. "Paradise belongs to my aunt. She owns it. Her father lived here, and her grandfather, ages and ages ago."

"He will," said the boy gleefully. "He's got a morbidge – bought it, he did, from a lawyer. She has to pay him money, regular, and she hasn't any. One day soon, he'll take the farm

and we'll move in. We'll join it to Starveall and make it the
biggest farm around. We'll take it all apart, and I'll find her
treasure."

"I think you're horrible," cried Verity, "and unkind." She
wanted to say how fat he was and rude to talk with a straw in his
mouth all the time, but that would be rude too. "You won't get
into Paradise; we shall keep it safe, and the treasure, and we'll
find the morbidge she's lost. And she will live here for ever and
ever and ever."

The boy opened his mouth to answer back, but at that
moment something happened. A large dog came up on the
Starveall side of the wall: a black dog with rough matted fur. It
spotted Verity and started to bark – the ragged, ferocious bark
that she had heard on the day she arrived.

A man came out of a building – a short, bulky man in dirty
clothes, with a sullen, unpleasant face. Black hair was plastered
down on his forehead. He looked up at the wall and shook his
fist.

"Get off there!" he shouted. The boy dropped clumsily down
the far side of the wall. Verity clambered down her own side. She
heard further shouting. "What you been doing? Who you been
talking to?" She felt an urge to run away and raced across the
empty yard, back to the door. She opened, closed, locked it and
walked away. She felt upset.

She had hoped to find something new and interesting
behind the Forbidden Door, but all she had seen was an ugly,
angry place. How nasty Starveall and its family must be. She had
stuck up for Aunt Esther, though – and then, with a sinking
heart, she realised what she had said. Aunt Esther had lost the
morbidge, and she, Verity, had told the boy it was lost! Suppose

he remembered that, and told his father. Would he remember? He had looked stupid, but also cunning. A feeling of misery swept over her.

After a time the garden worked its magic and she felt a little better. She went indoors. Aunt Esther had woken up from her nap, Samuel needed taking for a walk and there was lavender to be picked. Aunt Esther was so kind – and as the afternoon passed, the incident on the wall became less vivid. But it returned again when, in a quiet moment, she put the key into the drawer. Late that evening, as she stood at her open window, she heard once more, distant but ominous, the angry bark of the dog of Starveall Farm.

Three days passed. Nothing happened. Then, on the fourth day, when Verity and her aunt were making peppermints in the kitchen, the front doorbell rang. Jack went to answer it. Verity heard a distant voice – a loud, assertive voice it seemed – and Jack returned. He stood in the kitchen doorway, pointed southwards, sketched a well-built figure, drew his hand over his forehead, and looked glum.

"Oby Blagdon!" said Aunt Esther. "What does he want! You stay here, dear," and she swept out. There was a long pause, then raised voices could be heard from the hall. Jack gave Verity a significant look. Steps were heard. Aunt Esther emerged down the passage. She looked upset.

"Come and help me, dear," she said. "He's brought a paper that he wants me to read. I can't see it with my glasses on – you look at it and tell me."

Verity put down her spoon, wiped her hands and took off her apron. She followed her aunt to the hall. The visitor was standing in front of the empty fireplace. She recognised him at once – the angry farmer whom she had seen from the wall: well-built, aggressive, his legs planted firmly apart, his face red and his black hair plastered down on his forehead. His little black eyes fixed on Verity.

"This your heir?" he said. "I'm glad there's someone here to do your spelling for you."

"Read his paper for me, dear," said Aunt Esther, passing over a document which lay on the table. Verity looked at it. It was a large piece of parchment with a jagged top edge. The words in the first line were large, with lots of loops and twirls; the rest were in very small letters.

Oby Blagdon snatched at the parchment. "The material parts is this – look!" he said, thrusting out his lower lip. "This indenture dated … What's that say?" he demanded, holding it in front of Verity's face.

"It says the … the twentieth day of Au … August in the year of our Lord one thousand six hundred and sixty," she said.

"20 August 1660," he repeated. "Now read that!"

She looked at the place to which he pointed with his large, dirty finger. It was not easy to read. She said, "It looks like, 'for a term of fifty years'."

"They learned you well," said the farmer condescendingly. "And I'm learning her. This is her morbidge, what I bought lawfully from Reckitt. This morbidge falls due one month from now. If she pays me the two hundred pounds due, the morbidge is quit. If she doesn't, I take the property. It's as simple as that. I needn't have done nothing today. I could 'a come in here a month hence and turned her out. But I know my Christian duty, and I'm giving you time to make your arrangements. I'll be back in a month's time with my lawyer."

He coiled his document into a roll with his large red hands, and stamped out of the room.

Aunt Esther sat down on a bench. She looked old and careworn. "His father was civil enough," she said, "but I never could like that Oby, always shouting and putting people down and gathering money. He wants me out of here – I've long known that – but the morbidge lasts for ninety years, not fifty. If only I could find my copy to make sure."

Verity saw it all, very clearly. Her eyes filled with tears. "Oh Aunt Esther, it's my fault. I took the key of the log-yard door and I went in to look. And I saw a boy on the wall and he was rude to me and said that his father would turn you out of the farm. I said he wouldn't, and I said you'd find your treasure and your morbidge. Now the father knows you've lost your morbidge and he thinks he has you in his power. And I have caused all this." She started to cry.

"Bless the girl," said her aunt. "I wouldn't mind you going to the log yard. And as for you talking about me losing my morbidge, well, you weren't to know he'd come round causing trouble." She put her arms round Verity and kissed her. "You didn't tell any lies, that's what matters. Let's go back to the kitchen, and forget him. I'll work something out."

So they returned to the peppermints. But the charm of making sweets was over for Verity and the rest of the day was spoilt. She felt guilty – all the trouble was due to her. She looked at the picture of Eve as she went through the hall. Eve went where she wasn't supposed to go. She spoke to the Enemy and she and Adam were thrown out of Paradise. But that was simpler than this. Adam and Eve were punished, which balanced things.

Now, Verity would ride home on the cart and Aunt Esther, Jack and Tom would be thrown out of Paradise. Aunt Esther hadn't been cross but had forgiven her. Verity hadn't had any punishment to cancel out her wickedness.

The day dragged on. She made half-hearted attempts to look for the treasure. Her aunt seemed sad and conversation flagged. After supper in the parlour, Esther got up. "My head hurts, dear. I am going to bed. Maybe I'll be able to think better about all this in the morning." She said "goodnight" and left.

Verity remained in the parlour, deep in misery. If disaster were to be avoided, the missing morbidge had to be found at once, to check what it said. Finding the treasure would be better still. Then Oby Blagdon could be given his money, and Paradise would be free for ever. But how could she find either of these when everyone had searched so long and unsuccessfully? She looked around the room for ideas: oak furniture, blue plates, books. Her eyes rested on the big family Bible which lay on the chest of drawers. The Bible was a vast, mysterious thing – hundreds and hundreds of pages, full of incomprehensible names and stories. But it could tell you things. You put a key in the book at a certain place, then you tied up the book and held it by a piece of string. The book turned or dipped when you asked it questions. It would be easy to find a key, but she did not know where you put it in. More to the point, she had been told that putting the key into the Bible was wicked. It was a sort of witchcraft. That was no good; she was in bad enough trouble with God already.

Still, you could ask the Bible a good question, and then open it to see what the answer was. There would be no harm in that.

In fact, you could ask more than once. In stories, you were always allowed three questions – no more, no less – and you needed to be careful what you asked. She stood the Bible up, with its spine towards the window. Then she half opened the covers so that the pages stuck out like a fan. She closed her eyes and said, "What should we do?" She pushed her finger into the book, and looked at what she had touched. It was the middle of a sentence, and it said, "fear not, for I am with thee".

This was comforting – even encouraging. But it gave no clue to the morbidge or the treasure. She shut her eyes again and spoke her second question. "What will get us out of the morbidge?" Her finger moved forward towards the Bible. When she opened her eyes, she saw that it was pointing to five words at the back of the book: "he that hath the key".

This was puzzling. The Bible did not make it clear what the words were about, or who "he" was. The only clue lay in the word "key". Which key? There were dozens of keys in the drawer! It would take as long to work out what the keys were for as it would to search the whole of the house and garden for secret treasure.

She decided on a more direct approach. In stories, the last question was always the most important. She closed her eyes and said, very carefully, "Where is the treasure?" She pushed her finger towards the Bible, hoping to put it somewhere into the middle. But when she opened her eyes, it was again among the pages at the end. She looked at the print eagerly. It read:

Lay not up for yourselves treasures upon earth, where moth and rust doth corrupt, and where thieves break through and steal.

But lay up for yourselves treasures in heaven … For where

your treasure is, there will your heart be also.

This was really disappointing. There was no clue. Indeed, the message, if there was one, seemed to be that no treasure existed. She banged the book shut and laid it down again. The Bible had always baffled her, and it was no help now. The nearest it had come to being helpful was in talking about a key. "He that hath the key". What could that mean in "Paradise"? It could not refer to Jack, because he did not look after the keys. It could perhaps, mean the drawer where the keys were kept.

She pulled open the drawer. Like many things in the house, it stuck halfway. She had to give a hard tug before it squeaked and allowed itself to be dragged right out of the chest. She held it in both hands, and poured all the keys on the floor. There they were – several dozen of them, single and in bundles, labelled and unlabelled. Where did they belong? What did they open?

It was clear that the drawer had not been emptied for years. There was a lot of dust inside. She brushed off some with her hands and blew away more. The bottom of the drawer was lined with a plain brown sheet – "thicker than paper, possibly parchment," she thought. It was not quite even and bulged in one corner. Could there be something under it? The lining fitted the drawer tightly, and it was difficult to get a fingernail under the edge to lift it up, but eventually she did. The lining came out. There was nothing underneath except the base of the drawer. She was just about to put the lining back when she noticed that its other side was covered with writing. Part of it was folded, and when she unfolded it, she saw that one edge was not straight. Where had she seen such a thing before?

"It has a jagged top," she said to herself, "exactly like Oby's."

She started to read: "This indenture dated the thirteenth day of August in the year of our Lord … why, it's like the morbidge!

"And the aforementioned sum shall be redeemed," she read on, "within ninety years of this present date." Ninety years! The other one had said fifty. She remembered that well, because it had been difficult to read. It had looked rather faint, as if something had been scratched out and rewritten. In a minute, she was running upstairs to her aunt's bedroom.

Next morning, Aunt Esther seated herself in the parlour and, with much scratching of a pen and jabbing into the inkwell, wrote a letter to her lawyer asking him to call at Paradise. As soon as Mr Standish replied, agreeing the date, Jack was dispatched with a note to Starveall Farm, inviting Oby to come round to discuss the morbidge. The day came, the parlour was tidied and polished and a decanter of malmsey wine was put on the table with slices of plum cake. Unfortunately, Aunt Esther would not let Verity watch. "That Oby Blagdon's in the wrong," she said. "he couldn't wait for his money, so he altered the morbidge. But it doesn't do to triumph over people. The lawyer will handle him."

So Verity went to her bedroom, and looked through the window at the comings and goings. First, at eleven o'clock, came Mr Standish, her aunt's lawyer – a handsome white-haired man on a cob horse, which Tom took away to the stable while the lawyer went into the parlour for his wine. Then, at noon, the front gate was flung open and Oby Blagdon marched through with his plastered forelock, looking – thought Verity – both aggressive and uneasy. With him came a little man dressed in shabby black with a thin, cunning face, who was evidently his lawyer. They disappeared inside.

From what Verity heard afterwards, Mr Standish asked Oby to lay his copy of the morbidge on the table, produced the other and fitted the two together. "At which Oby's eyes fair jumped out of his head," said Aunt Esther. Mr Standish invited Oby and his lawyer to check that the documents were the genuine halves of the morbidge, to which they muttered agreement, and then pointed out the difference in the date when the morbidge fell due. "Yours," he said to Oby, "has been altered."

"Are you accusing me of forgery?" shouted Oby.

"I am accusing you of nothing," replied Mr Standish. "I merely say that your document is not correct and that the mortgage has another forty years to run. If you agree, we will draw up a statement to that effect, and that will be the end of the matter."

Oby swallowed several times – "He was quiet for five minutes," said Aunt Esther, "longer than I've ever known him" – and then he looked at his lawyer, who gave him a small, significant nod. The statement was drawn up, signed and witnessed, and Oby strode from the house with his lawyer after him. He did not even bang the gate behind him.

Verity looked down and saw him go. So Paradise was safe. She had endangered it, and she had saved it (no, help had come) out of the very same drawer. How odd that the morbidge had been in such an obvious spot, yet nobody had seen it. She turned to thinking about the treasure. Suppose that too was somewhere that everyone could see and no one noticed. What had been the answer to the third question? "Lay not up … treasures upon earth … But treasures in heaven." What sort of treasures were they, and where would they be hidden? She sat for some time pondering this, until she heard her aunt's voice calling her downstairs.

There was a most joyful dinner in the hall with a roast chicken, followed by summer pudding and cream. Aunt Esther sat at the head of the table, Mr Standish on her right, Verity on her left, and Jack and Tom a little lower down. The lawyer raised his glass. "To Paradise!" he said. "And may it always remain."

"To Paradise!" they cried. Jack said nothing, but he grinned.

The carrier's cart stood at the gate again. Verity's box went up with bunches of roses and lavender for her mother, pots of jam and marmalade, and a box of peppermints for her brother. Verity shook hands with Jack and Tom and thanked them properly, hugged her aunt, and promised to come again.

"Next time, dear," said her aunt, 'we'll have a good look for the treasure! You know now that it's somewhere hereabouts."

Verity looked at the old house and the garden, at Jack and Tom and her aunt. "Yes, dear aunt," she said. "I do believe that it is."

Chapter 6

THE POACHER AND THE PIE

The Brierleigh postman walked up the drive of the Manor House, crunching the gravel with his boots and whistling "Home Sweet Home". He felt happy. It was a fine sunny day in October and warm for the time of year. Tomorrow was Saturday, the day of the village feast, with a fair, side-stalls, morris men, dancing in the evening and the pub open all hours. He finished work at twelve and for the rest of the day he was going to enjoy himself.

He took out a handful of letters for Mr and Mrs Fursdon and postcards for Miss Mercia and Master George. He pushed them through the big, brass letterbox – and pulled out his hand in alarm. There was a vicious growl from the other side of the door, the snarl of a large savage animal. Something dragged the letters through the box. There was a sound of wet jaws slavering and chewing. The postman scratched his head. Should he ring the bell and say that the dog had got the letters? No fear! If someone opened the door, that dog would be out in a moment, biting his trousers. Better to go and say nothing. Odd though; there was an old dog lying on the lawn, asleep in the sun. Were there two dogs? He walked back down the drive, with a puzzled frown.

A thick red curtain hung inside the door. It moved a little, and a boy's face looked out. The curtain was to stop draughts coming in and Georgie had often blessed his mother's dislike of the cold. You could hide between the curtain and the door without anyone knowing, which was specially useful after bedtime when you were supposed to have gone upstairs but really hadn't! He changed from being a wolf to an Indian scout. Placing the letters on the hall table, he leapt upstairs in large, silent jumps, carefully missing out the sixth stair and the thirteenth, which creaked. He raced along the upstairs landing and burst through the door of the schoolroom.

Mercia sat in her wheelchair, just as she had done each morning for the last three years. The wheelchair was one of the new-fangled kind which you could work yourself by means of a circle of steel fixed on to each of the two main wheels. Mercia had had the furniture in the room arranged so that she could wheel herself from window to window. She could travel pretty fast: she had already seen the postman come and go. Normally, on a Friday morning like this, Mercia and Georgie had lessons in the schoolroom from their governess who did not allow it to be used as a cycle track, but this lady – the aptly named Miss Fortune – was the victim of every cold which came to Brierleigh. Today, she was lying in her bedroom with a sore throat and a large box of Perkins' Patent Lozenges.

"Oh, Georgie, you gave me a fright!" complained his sister. Georgie, after creeping silently into the room, had given a war-whoop in the best Indian manner.

"We've got two postcards with foreign stamps on," announced Georgie, "and I hid behind the door and frightened the postman. He had an awful shock. Bags I the stamps for my album."

"I don't suppose you even know where the postcards come from, let alone reading the writing," said Mercia. "Hand them over, and I'll tell you."

Georgie made a face. Geography and reading were not his favourite subjects and he had not even started foreign languages. Mercia was already well advanced in French and German.

"The postcards are from Uncle Septimus and Aunt Agatha, who are staying in Ostend," she announced. "It's in Belgium."

"What do they say?" asked Georgie.

"Mine says, 'We are staying in a pleasant hotel and have bathed twice.' Yours says, 'We have listened to the band and watched the soldiers drill.' Very dull. You can take them, and soak off the stamps. But do not let Mamma see them, or we shall be made to write thank-you letters."

Georgie stuffed the postcards into his pocket.

"There is something more important to discuss," said Mercia. "I have been watching the windows since half past eight, and I have not seen Sam. Have you?"

"No," said Georgie. "I went down the drive three times before the postman came. There's no sign of him."

"Sam really is most vexing," said Mercia firmly. "I told him to come without fail, straight after breakfast. Mrs Burnham was to let him in by the kitchen door, and he was to creep up the back staircase."

Sam Handwich lived in the village. He wasn't strong enough for regular work (nasty people said he was too lazy). He did odd jobs, ran messages and fetched things. Sometimes, he went into the woods and came back with a fat rabbit. But a year ago, when Sam had last appeared in court for poaching, Mr Fursdon (who was a magistrate in the police court) had warned him severely that next time he would be sent to prison. Since then, Sam had been very careful.

Mercia had met Sam when Georgie was pushing her chair round the village. He was standing outside his cottage. Unlike so many people who felt embarrassed by a girl in a wheelchair, Sam behaved quite normally. He had an amusing way of talking and was a great teller of improbable stories about himself. Mercia had become interested in his family: his wife and his four children. She had told him that he must never go poaching again. Sam had solemnly promised he wouldn't. In return, Mercia had told her governess about him, and Miss Fortune, who did good works in the village, had given him tickets for free blankets and free coal.

Then Mercia and Georgie decided they wanted a rabbit. They would keep it in the stables, and Georgie would feed it on dandelion leaves and whatever else rabbits liked. Sam had promised to find one for a shilling and Georgie had gone down twice to Sam's cottage to see if it had arrived. The second time, yesterday evening, Sam had promised to deliver the animal to the schoolroom after breakfast, having been warned that Miss Fortune would not be there.

"It's no good, Georgie," said Mercia firmly. "Today is too good a day to waste, with the Misfortune out of the way. You will have to go down again and ask him for it."

"I can't go now," said Georgie with his eye on the door. "Papa and Mamma are coming!"

There was a sound of feet on the staircase and a murmur of voices. The door opened and in came Mr George Fursdon senior, the magistrate, and Mrs Fursdon. They kissed Mercia, and stood in the middle of the room, very upright and solid. Mr Fursdon had a solemn way of talking, as though he was in the police court.

"You are lucky to have an extra holiday," he observed, in the voice he used for letting off a tramp with a caution. "I hope you will not be bored without any school."

"No indeed, Papa," said Mercia hastily, fearing that some tasks might be suggested. "We have lots to read."

"I do not think you need stay in the schoolroom today," said Mrs Fursdon, who was rather querulous. "It is very cold here. You would be better downstairs by the fire and you could help me wind some wool for my knitting."

"Thank you, Mamma," said Mercia. "I will certainly help you later on, but I would prefer to stay here this morning. We are very excited about the Feast and we are making menus and placecards for the guests who are coming to lunch tomorrow."

"I am not sure that the Feast is a very good thing for the village," said her mother. "It is so noisy and attracts the most undesirable people. I think it encourages drinking and crimes."

"Oh, I do not see any great harm in it, my dear," said the magistrate. "It brings the village together. In fact, I have arranged for something special to happen today in connection with the Feast, which I hope you will both enjoy very much."

"What is it, Papa?" asked Georgie, springing to attention. He had been keeping quiet in case schoolwork was mentioned.

"I have arranged for the Brierleigh mummers to visit our house," declared Mr Fursdon importantly. "It is, of course, difficult for Mercia to see them, so they will come here and dance and act their play at half past six tonight. We can watch them from the staircase. And afterwards, I have asked Burnham to serve them some cakes and mulled wine before they go on their way."

"The village mummers!" exclaimed Mrs Fursdon. "I am not sure that they are very reliable or proper. They are organised by Handwich, who is a notoriously low character in the village."

"Do not worry, my dear," replied her husband soothingly. "Mumming is a good, old-fashioned entertainment, and as for Handwich, I am sure he will behave himself. The last time he was in the police court for poaching, I told him that I would deal with him very severely if he ever stepped out of line again. He is always very polite now when he sees me."

Mercia thought it was high time to back her father. "It is a lovely idea, Papa, and you are very kind to think of Georgie and me. We have never seen the mummers and we should like to watch the play." As she was speaking, she heard a ringing noise in the distance – the sound of the kitchen doorbell. Could it be Sam? Mercia hoped he would have more sense than to come upstairs while her parents were there!

"Well, I suppose it will do no harm in the hall," said Mrs Fursdon doubtfully. "But they must not mark the floor with their boots. And I do wish, George, that you had consulted me about their refreshments. Mrs Burnham is already very busy with our luncheon party tomorrow and she will not be pleased with extra work. And that reminds me: I am worried about our catering. We have so any people coming to meals."

"Why, dear,' replied her husband, "surely we had a large order from the grocer's yesterday?"

"Yes, we did, but when I examined it, I found that several things had been forgotten. We have a party of ten tomorrow, the Aclands and the vicar on Sunday and the magistrates to lunch on Monday, not to mention anyone who might come in from the village."

Mr Fursdon prided himself on solving problems. "That is easily dealt with," he said, rubbing his hands. "Write another order to the grocer's: a large pie, a ham, some cakes, puddings, candied fruits, and so forth. The groom can ride into Ayster this afternoon and get them."

Mrs Fursdon opened her mouth to object but at that moment there was an interruption. A loud knock sounded on the door. The red-faced cook, Mrs Burnham, burst into the room.

"Begging your pardon, sir, for interrupting, but there's a perliceman at the door, asking to see you urgently, and my leg's in the oven." Georgie giggled.

"A policeman!" said the magistrate with surprise. "I wonder why – perhaps he wants instructions about the Feast. Show him into the library, Burnham, and say that I will come down immediately. I must go now, children, but I will see you later." He marched downstairs.

Mrs Fursdon went too. "I ought to think about my list for the grocer's," she said. "It is such a worry – there are so many things we might need." Mercia and Georgie were left on their own.

"A policeman!" repeated Mercia, who liked to know about everything that went on. "That sounds interesting. Georgie, go down and listen outside the library door. Then come back and report."

"Sir!" said Georgie, saluting. He was now a ranger, scouting to spy on the enemy. He tiptoed quietly down the staircase, avoiding the two creaky stairs, and crept beneath the table in the hall. This was just outside the library door and the door was half open. He peeped around the doorway and almost gasped. In the narrow shaft of his vision, he could see Sam Handwich and part of a very large policeman.

"What is the meaning of this?" his father was saying.

"It's an arrest, sir," said the policeman. "Open and shut case. Flagrant poaching in Lord Fitzpaine's woods."

"Explain," came the voice of his father.

The policeman searched his uniform for his notebook. At last he found it and began to speak in a droning voice. "I were proceeding in a southerly direction up Berry Hill, sir, at eight o'clock this morning when I caught sight of a movement and a rustling in the bushes. I hinvestigated and discovered the accused, crouching down and trying not to be seen. He had a canvas bag containing two brace of pheasants. I arrested him and his bag and, in view of your instructions about poachers, I brought him straight to your house."

"You acted correctly, constable," came the voice of the magistrate. "Handwich, what have you to say for yourself?"

Sam's voice floated out, both eager and ingratiating. "Oh, there's an explanation, sir. I can explain everything. This morning, sir, being a bright sunny morning, I got up very early and went out, sir, to take some exercise. While I was walking on the Ayster road, I was overtaken by a horse and cart and at the very moment that they passed me, the wheels went over a stone and something fell off the back. I looked at it, and found it was two brace of pheasants. I shouted to the driver, but he didn't hear me, so I picked up the pheasants intending to ask who they belonged to. Then I walked through Lord Fitzpaine's woods by the public footpath and tripped over a snare which someone had thoughtlessly placed there for catching rabbits. It was at this point that Constable arrested me."

There was a pause. Sam added, "That's all, sir."

"Handwich! Handwich!" came the stern voice of the magistrate. "I have been in the police court now for – seventeen years. I heard the story about pheasants falling off the back of a cart from the first poacher I ever convicted, and I have heard it

about twice a month ever since. You are a notorious poacher –
have been in front of me four or five times to my knowledge –
and the last time I told you that if you poached again, I would
deal with you very severely. This I shall now do. Today is Friday.
The next meeting of the police court is on Thursday. As there is
no police station in the village, I am going to send you to prison
in the city on remand, for six days, until your case comes up in
the court."

There was clear panic in Sam's voice. "But sir, I shall miss the
village Feast! I'm organising the mummers and the play!"

"You should have thought of that," said Mr Fursdon firmly,
"before you went poaching. Let me see. There is a train to the
city in one hour. I will write out the order and while I am doing
so, constable, you can take Handwich into the kitchen, where
Mrs Burnham will give you some refreshment – but Handwich is
not to have anything."

Sam broke in breathlessly. "I think I'd better tell you the real
story, sir."

"The real story?" said the magistrate scornfully. "Oh, you are
a great storyteller, Handwich! No, I will not discuss the matter
further. Law and order must be kept and justice must be done.
It is my duty to see to it. Constable Clumber will take you to
prison on the eleven o'clock train."

"What shall I do with the bag, sir?" asked Clumber.

"We shall need that as evidence," said Mr Fursdon. "You can
leave it in the stables and take it to the police station later."

The library door opened and Georgie shrank closer beneath
the table. He saw the blue trouser legs of the policeman go past,
then Sam's frayed trouser legs, and felt the floorboards tremble
as the two men marched across the hall and down the passage to

the kitchen. He peered out cautiously. His father had closed the library door and was evidently writing inside. Georgie wriggled from his hiding place. He tiptoed down the kitchen passage, just as Sam was following Clumber into the kitchen. Sam turned and saw him.

"I didn't do it, Master George," he called. "Tell Miss Mercy that." Before Georgie could reply, Clumber turned and pulled Sam into the kitchen. The door shut.

Georgie ran quickly back to the hall, leapt silently up the stairs and burst into the schoolroom.

"Mercy! Something awful has happened! The policeman has arrested Sam! He was caught poaching – he had goodness knows how many pheasants with him! Papa is very angry and he has sent him to prison for a week."

"He can't!" said Mercia. "He can only do that in the police court."

"He has," said Georgie. "He's put him 'on command' or something, until the police court meets on Thursday. The policeman is taking him to prison on the next train. I saw Sam for just a moment before he went into the kitchen and he said he didn't do it. He said, tell you."

Mercia thought for a moment. "If he said that, it's true. I wonder what we can do. I think you had better ask Papa to come up and see me." Georgie dashed off down the stairs. "Sam is naughty," she thought. "He's always up to things. But he did promise he wouldn't poach again and I believe him. Perhaps he was up in the woods looking for that rabbit. In that case it's partly my fault. Why does Papa have to be so hard? Why couldn't he let it go until the police court meets next week?"

A few minutes later, her father came in through the door,

followed by Georgie. Mercia said, "Papa, Georgie says that Sam has been caught poaching. I'm afraid it's my fault. You see, I asked him to find us a live pet rabbit. We thought we could keep it in the stables. I promised him a shilling for one and I never thought that he would go poaching for it."

"It is good of you to accept the blame, Mercia," said her father, "but the facts are that Handwich was found with two brace of pheasants, not a rabbit. He is a notorious poacher, and I warned him last time that if he was caught again, I would deal with him very severely."

"But it is Feast day tomorrow, Papa," said Mercia. "Can he not stay at home until the police court meets? His wife is not well and they have small children."

Her father thrust out his chin. "Justice must be done. You might make an exception in a special case, but not for a hardened poacher – a regular offender. I have to see that justice is done and seen to be done. I have written out the order and he is going to prison on the next train. This means that the mummers will not come tonight. I am sorry to disappoint you, but I have to do my duty – before God and the Law." He saw that his daughter was about to reply, and stopped her by leaving the room.

"It's beastly unfair," said Georgie. "The mummers aren't coming and the Feast will be spoilt."

"That's not really the point," said Mercia. "The point is that Sam said he didn't do it and he asked us to believe him. And I do. This calls for desperate remedies. We must save Sam, somehow."

"I know," proposed Georgie, "I'll get some village boys and rescue him while the policeman is taking him to the railway station."

Mercia thought for a while. "No, he would recognise you and there would be worse trouble. But I have a sort of an idea. Go downstairs, Georgie, and see what is happening. When Papa writes letters, he usually leaves them on the hall table. See what is there, and bring the letters to me, very quickly."

Georgie surpassed himself, and came back with a handful of letters in just over twenty seconds. "There were lots of them," he panted, "and I could not tell which was which, so I brought them all."

"Oh, Georgie," said Mercia with a laugh, "when will you improve with your reading? Let me see. These are quite clearly in Papa's writing and these are in Mamma's. Now, I shall need two envelopes. There are some in the drawer in the hall table." Georgie disappeared again and Mercia turned her wheelchair round and moved it to the schoolroom table. There were pens on the table and an inkwell. "Give me the envelopes," she said when her brother returned, "and turn round and look at the door. Then, if anyone asks you about this later, you can tell the truth and say you know nothing about it." There were little tearing sounds and the scratching of a pen. "Turn round now, Georgie," said his sister, "and put back the letters quickly, before someone finds they have gone."

"But what will happen?" asked Georgie. "Will Sam go to prison?"

"You will just have to see," said Mercia, and she giggled. "Put the letters straight back and, as you have been so kind and helpful, I am going to tell you a special new ghost story this afternoon."

Ten minutes later, Mercia looked out of the window and saw Sam Handwich disappearing down the drive, his arm in the grip of the ponderous Constable Clumber. About twenty minutes after that she noticed, in the far distance, a little white cloud of smoke moving south across the fields. It was the eleven o'clock train on its way to the city!

Mr Fursdon spent the rest of the morning in the library. He had several more letters to write. Every so often he stopped, glanced out of the window, and smiled. Well, he had certainly taught one poacher a lesson! When people heard how he treated poachers, there would be a lot less poaching in this district! He rubbed his hands again and poured himself a glass of sherry wine.

He had lunch with the family. This was rather gloomy. Mercia and Georgie were quiet and his wife spent most of the time describing the grocery list she had sent. After lunch, he felt bored and decided to go for a ride, so he changed into his riding clothes and went round to the stables. There, hanging up, was the bag which Clumber had found with Handwich. He looked inside. No doubt about it! Four pheasants, plump ones too. He put back the bag with satisfaction and took out Cato his horse for a trot round the lanes. He ambled slowly along, thinking about the punishments for really bad poachers. He would have to look them up in his magistrate's book.

By the time he returned, it was past four o'clock. He handed over the horse to the stable boy and walked round to the front of the house, to make sure that the garden was tidy. Tut! Tut! There were two – three – small weeds in the drive, which the gardener should have noticed. But what was that? – a noise of horses in the road. He walked to the front of the garden to look out. A man came into sight in faultless riding attire, on a magnificent Arab stallion. It was Lord Fitzpaine himself, riding

Sultan. His groom on a less imposing horse, followed a few paces behind him.

"Hello, Fursdon," called the earl. "Good day for a ride, what? How's the poaching?"

Mr Fursdon bounded forward eagerly. "My Lord!" he cried. "I've dealt with one today. Caught on your very own property. I've just been writing a note to tell you."

"What! Bagged one of the bounders who've been plaguing me?" said the earl. "Who caught him? None of my men reported anything."

"Constable Clumber brought him in this morning," said Mr Fursdon. "Fellow from this village. Handwich."

The earl whistled. "By Gad. He's an old offender, isn't he? Anything on him?"

"Two brace of pheasants," said the magistrate. "They're in my stable."

The earl slid down from the saddle and gave his reins to the groom. "Let's see," he said. "I always like to know what these fellows are after."

They walked round the house to the stables. Mr Fursdon took down the bag and held it open triumphantly. The earl peered in.

"Handsome birds, Fursdon," he said. He gave a snort. "Only trouble is, they aren't mine."

"What!" said the magistrate.

"Absolutely not. This is a fancy variety. Golden Wonders. We don't rear 'em. Wherever your poacher found 'em it wasn't my woods."

"Are you sure?" asked Mr Fursdon incredulously.

"Quite. Nobody round here has 'em. The Duke does, but

that's forty miles away. If your poacher bagged 'em there, he's working on a pretty big scale."

The earl was losing interest. "Got to go," he said. "Countess wants me. Dinner party." He strode off. The magistrate dropped the bag and scurried after him, anxious to escort his lordship from the premises in the proper fashion. The earl remounted his horse, gave a casual wave and set off at a fast pace with the groom in pursuit.

Mr Fursdon was left on the lawn in confusion. He felt upset. That stupid man Clumber had not examined the bag properly! But then, neither had he, the magistrate! He suddenly realised that he had been hasty with Handwich, even unjust. Handwich was now in prison, waiting to be tried for a crime that he might not have committed. There was nothing else for it. He would have to get Handwich out of prison again. If he went to the post office, he could send a message to the prison by telegram, asking for Handwich to be released. He would look foolish to the governor, but it could not be helped. He must do everything that was right.

He went into the house, found some money and walked briskly to the village post office. He sent his telegram with the words, "KINDLY RELEASE HANDWICH IMMEDIATELY. LETTER FOLLOWS. FURSDON." He returned home and as he passed the sitting room he heard voices. One voice seemed oddly familiar. Who was it? He turned the handle of the door, and entered.

Mercia and Georgie had settled themselves in the sitting room, in the quiet period which followed afternoon tea. Their father was out riding, and their mother was discussing groceries and menus with the housekeeper. Mercia was in the full flood of her ghost story.

"The two children were left alone in the haunted house. The moonlight shone through the curtainless windows with a ghastly – ghastly – ghastly radiance. There were mysterious creaking sounds!"

Georgie leant forwards, hugging his knees, his eyes growing bigger and bigger.

"There was a strange noise," said Mercia, putting an eerie tone into her voice, "like the sound of fingers tapping at a window." She gave a start. "Whatever was that noise?"

Georgie listened. "It's a tapping noise, on the window." He dropped his voice to a whisper. "There's someone outside!"

"Go and see what it is," said Mercia.

Georgie got up stealthily and peeped round the edge of the window. The lamps in the room made it hard to see outside in the fading light. He loosened the catch and pushed the window up. "Aha!" he said. "A poacher!" There was a movement from outside, and a head poked in.

"Sam!" cried Mercia. "Where have you sprung from? Georgie, let him in, then shut the window." Sam vaulted dexterously over the window sill. Georgie closed the window and drew the curtains across it. Sam stood in the centre of the room. He had a grin on his face, both guilty and triumphant.

"You are looking rather pleased with yourself, Sam," said Mercia.

Sam drew himself up. "Well I would, wouldn't I, Miss, escaping from prison!"

"And how did you do that, pray?" asked Mercia, raising her eyebrows.

Sam tapped the side of his nose. "Those prison bars," he said, "very badly made nowadays. Bend in your fingers. Good strong sheets they have, though. All you have to do is tie them to the end of the bed, slide down into the yard and walk out of the front door. Nobody even notices you going."

"Sam!" said Mercia, raising her finger. "You are not telling the truth!"

Sam blushed. "Well, no, Miss," he said, "but it makes a good story, like the one you were telling just now."

"I know perfectly well that you never went to prison," said Mercia. "The governor would not have you, would he?"

"Well, no, Miss," said Sam apologetically. "It was very funny like, what happened."

"Sam Handwich," said Mercia severely, "what was going on up Berry Hill this morning?"

Sam smiled. "Well, it was all most misfortunate, Miss. Early this morning, I happened to be out on business, taking some pheasants to somebody. I was taking a short cut through the wood when Constable caught me. I didn't want to say where the pheasants came from – it's rather complicated – so I panicked and made up one of my stories. Mr Fursdon, he got angry and sent me off to prison straightaway."

"And what happened when you arrived?" said Mercia.

Sam looked at her, cunningly. "Strange, wasn't it? The policeman had a letter with him – with your father's writing on the envelope. He gave it to the governor and the governor started laughing. Governor said, 'It's an order for a big pie and so forth. All we supply here,' he said, 'is rocks and mailbags.' Then Clumber asked what we should do, and the governor said, 'Go home'."

Sam gave her a shrewd look. "Now, Miss, how d'you think that letter got into that envelope?"

This time it was Mercia's turn to blush. She was wondering what to say when her ear caught the sound of footsteps outside the door. "It's Papa," she said. "Quick, hide behind the sofa!" Sam dived out of sight.

The door opened and Mr Fursdon entered. He glanced at his children keenly. "Mercia, Georgie, you look pale. I hope you are not angry with me about the mummers."

"No, Papa," said Mercia, "but we are still very upset about Sam Handwich being sent to prison."

"I see," said the magistrate. He paused, wondering how to break the news. A father couldn't apologise to his own children. "There seems to have been a mistake," he said at last. "I have asked for Handwich to be released from the prison."

"Oh, good," said Mercia. "I knew he hadn't done it."

"Knew?" said her father. "How did you know?"

"He said so, and I believed him," said Mercia.

"You have to be very careful, in my position," said Mr Fursdon solemnly, "about believing what people tell you."

"Yes, Papa," said Mercia, "but how should we get on if we don't believe anything people say? Especially poor people – they don't have other people to speak for them."

"I am concerned about the poor," said her father. "I help to pay for the free coal and free blankets."

"Those things are very useful, Papa," said Mercia, "but the poor need us to believe in them too, to help them take courage and get through their difficulties."

Mr Fursdon couldn't think what to say. His daughter was talking like the vicar. He cleared his throat. "Well, perhaps that is right," he said. "I must admit that if I had Handwich in front of me now, I wouldn't do what I did this morning."

Mercia's eyes sparkled. "That is easily arranged," she said. She waved her hand as if she were a conjuror at a children's party. "Stand up, Sam!"

Sam immediately appeared behind the sofa. He bowed slightly and tugged his forelock.

"Good heavens!" cried the magistrate. "Handwich! In my drawing room!" Thoughts raced through his head. "But I have only just asked the prison to let you out. How on earth are you here?"

Sam thought it wise to change the subject. "Begging your pardon, sir, but I promised Miss Mercy a live pet rabbit – which I have got here – and I said, come what may, she would have it by the Feast." He put his hand into a large pocket and pulled out a small brown rabbit. Georgie ran over and started to stroke it.

Mr Fursdon still seemed dazed with surprise. "Handwich," he said, "how did you get out of prison? This is extraordinary!"

Sam licked his lips. He was just about to make up another story, when there was a second interruption. The door opened, and in came Mrs Fursdon. She was far too agitated to notice who else was there.

"Oh, my dear," said the lady, "there is such an upset in the kitchen, and all my arrangements are disorganised. The groom has just come back from Ayster, and he says he could not get the grocery order!"

Sam straightened himself, bowed to Mrs Fursdon, and said hastily, "Begging your pardon, sir, and compliments to you, ma'am and to Miss Fursdon and Master Fursdon, but I shall have to leave now to organise the mummers." He tugged his forelock again and went out through the door.

"Oh!" exclaimed Mrs Fursdon. "However did that man Handwich come into our sitting room?"

"I have been asking the same question," said her husband. "But what is this about the grocery order?"

"Why," said his wife, "I gave my list to the groom, but the silly man says that when he arrived at the shop there was no list in the envelope. There was some other sort of letter. And they said that someone had already been in and collected our groceries. Such nonsense! Now I am left without any of the things I wanted."

Mr Fursdon opened his mouth to say something, but at this moment a third interruption occurred. It was the sound of a great knocking at the front door. Boom! Boom! Boom!

His wife jumped. "Whatever is that noise?" she exclaimed.

"It means, Mamma," said Mercia, "that the mummers have come in the nick of time for us all." Voices could be heard in the hall. There was a stamping of feet and a jingle of little bells. "May we go into the hall?" said Mercia, with sudden eagerness. She began to propel her chair forwards. Reluctantly, her parents followed her.

They arranged themselves in the hall: Mercia and her mother in chairs, Georgie on the stairs and their father standing. The postman played the fiddle, the mummers danced and then there was the play. Sam appeared as St George, wearing a suit of armour made of pasteboard. He fought a duel with the Turk and won, in terrific style. Georgie and Mercia clapped and clapped.

Mr Fursdon watched, but his mind kept wandering. He was thinking about the pheasants in the stables. Towards the end of the play, he slipped away and went across the yard. The groom was talking to the stable boy.

"A waste of time it was," the groom was complaining. "She give me this envelope to take to the grocer's and when I got there the shopman said, 'This isn't an order. It's something to do with the prison. Anyway,' he said, 'I thought we did an order for you a couple of hours ago. A big pie.' I said, 'No one else has been in.' I had to come back all the way for nothing and didn't I get a telling off from the mistress!"

He broke off quickly, as his master approached. "Good evening, sir! That bag, sir? Yes – hanging up in there. At least, it was. Jim – you seen that bag? Funny, sir, it was there half an hour ago. I know because I heard the mummers inside the house, and I noticed it then. No sir, Handwich hasn't been here, nor no one. Jim and me, we've been around all the time."

Mr Fursdon retired to the house, baffled. He came back into the hall, intending to speak to Handwich when the play finished. But the hall was empty. The mummers had gone. He called to Georgie who was climbing the stairs and asked where they were.

"Mamma sent them down to the kitchen for their wine and mince pies," said Georgie. "She said their boots were making a mark on the floor." He disappeared along the landing.

Mr Fursdon stood in the silent hall. He was absolutely mystified. He ticked things off, on his fingers. There were the stolen pheasants that hadn't been stolen. Then the prisoner, who had got out of prison before the telegram came. There was the grocery order that hadn't been an order and now the bag had gone – while Handwich was in the house! What did it all mean? He walked along the passage that led to the kitchen. There seemed to be a party in full swing on the other side of the kitchen door. He could hear Sam loudly telling a story, the cook screaming with laughter and guffaws from the mummers. He thought to himself, "I sent him to prison this morning, and now he's having the time of his life in my kitchen!" He took a pace towards the door, and thought better of it. He quietly walked away.

Later that evening, Mercia was in bed with her candle alight, when Georgie padded in.

"It's been a tremendous day," he said. "We didn't have school, Sam escaped going to prison and we watched the mummers." He paused and said, "What did you do to the letters?"

"You must work it out," replied Mercia, "from what happened."

"What does Sam do?" asked Georgie. "Is he really a poacher?"

"He can't do proper work," said Mercia. "He has a sort of makeshift life. But he's a free spirit. He comes and goes as he likes." She looked away. Then she said, in a bright voice, "Draw back the curtains, so I can look at the stars. And make sure that you wake up early tomorrow. We have to make a proper hutch for the rabbit – and when the Feast begins I want to see everything!"

Chapter 7

THE WHITE BIRD RETURNS

Mum, Chrissie and Aggro – three-quarters of the Smart family – were standing in Ayster High Street. It was early afternoon on Christmas Eve. The sky was overcast and there was a cold wind blowing. Some of the shops still had their Christmas decorations, but these were showing signs of wearing out: paperchains were dusty, Santa Clauses peeling at the edges. In other shops Christmas was already over. Windows were being changed and new posters were going up in bright colours, with SALE! SALE! SALE! in capital letters and exclamation marks.

Aggro was keeping up an incessant chatter. "Mum, can I have some crisps? Mum, can I have some ice cream? Mum, there's a gun in that window." A note of complaint crept into his voice. "Mum, when are we buying our presents?"

Mum, who was holding three bags, was in a bad mood. "Oh, Aggro," she said, "you've had crisps already. And you can't buy your presents until your Dad gets here. He's got your money."

Aggro, finding that no more crisps were available, changed into a soldier. "I'm Aggro of the SAS," he chanted. "Everyone in the street's a terrorist. Ack-ack-ack-ack-ack!" His real name was Andrew, but he had called himself Aggro since he first talked, and everyone agreed that it was a suitable change. He sprayed an imaginary sub-machine gun down the street and wiped out the last of the Christmas shoppers.

Mum lost some more of her temper. "Stop that noise!" she said. "Your Dad's late, and it's freezing. And I'm booked in for my hair at two o'clock."

Chrissie was staring at a poster across the road. "Mum," she said, "what's communion?" She pronounced it to rhyme with "onion".

"What's coming on where?" said Mum.

"Not coming on – communion," said Chrissie. "On that notice." She pointed to it. It said, "Holy Communion, 9.30."

"Oh, that," said Mum. "That's a church. It's something they do. Like singing."

"You ever been in a church, Mum?" asked Chrissie, reflectively.

"Only when we were married," said Mum. "We chose a nicer one than that, though – for the photos."

Aggro made a face. "Churches are yuk. Wayne Forrest goes to church. His parents take him. When he plays football, he falls over his laces."

"Can we look inside?" said Chrissie hopefully. She thought it unlikely and she was right.

"Not now, thank you!" said Mum. She gave a shout. "Rob! Over here. It's your Dad – at last." She picked up her bags, and prepared to move off.

Dad, who had been sauntering along on the opposite pavement, strolled across the road in front of a bus, got an angry hoot from the driver and waved back in a cheeky manner. "'Allo, 'allo, 'allo. Aggro, Chrissie. Mmm." He blew a kiss to his wife. "Here I come, haven't got a crumb. Spent all my money, and can I have some?" He held out his hand.

Mum looked cross. "I can't give you any," she said. "I'm short and I've still got to pay for my hair and my manicure."

Dad looked shifty. "Yeah. Well," he said, "it's been an

expensive morning. I spent a fair bit on the Christmas booze and the gee-gees were in a bad mood today."

Mum came back at him. "You said you'd get them their presents. I've got my shopping to finish and I'm booked in for my hair in half an hour."

Dad decided clowning was the best way out. He gave the family a jumbo-sized grin. "Don't sob, Rob'll do the job. Get yourself a credit card, and spend a few bob!" He thrust his hand into a pocket, and flourished a plastic card. "Always trust Rob Smart! Here you are, everybody! Let's spend, spend, spend!"

Mum stared at him suspiciously. "I thought you said our cards were all used up."

"Oh no," said Dad airily. "There's still a bit left on this one. You go off and get your hair done, luv. I'll take the kids down Sainsworth's – they got all the big toys there."

They left Mum and her bags and started to walk down the High Street. It was crowded, and as they turned into the shopping centre they met an obstruction. A brass band was stationed by the entrance, furiously blowing "See Amid the Winter Snow". Several young men and women were vigorously shaking tins at the shoppers, in aid of a charity. Dad passed them by, with his chin in the air as if he were considering the weather prospects, but the crowd forced him to stop in front of a vicar, with his collar on back to front and the biggest tin of all.

"Happy Christmas, sir," said the vicar. "We're collecting for Christmas charities." He smiled and held out the tin.

"So am I, squire," said Dad, pushing past. He called out, over his shoulder, "I'm collecting for the Rob Smart Christmas Beer and Horses Appeal. Come on, you kids." Aggro followed. Chrissie blushed.

"Dad," said Aggro. "Why are vicars always asking for money?"

"Got nothing else to do, lad," said his father.

"They're wimps, aren't they?" said Aggro.

"Oh, we had them in the army," said Dad. "Church parades on Sundays. Wittering away. We used to play poker in the back row."

"Was that when you were in Special Operations?" asked Aggro.

"That's right, kid. My operations are always special. Here we are. Sainsworth's. In we go."

They got on the escalators and rode to the toy department. The kids knew what their big presents were going to be. Chrissie was getting a new bike, Aggro a new football strip, boots, and computer games. He played in the school first eleven. Today, they were looking for extra presents, paid for by their auntie. Chrissie had kept her share of the money herself. Aggro's share, for some odd reason, had got into Dad's possession and been spent in the pub some weeks ago. Afterwards, Dad had promised to make amends and take them shopping to get what they wanted. He'd left it very late. On Saturdays he was busy, or said he was, at the second-hand car firm where he worked. Now it was Christmas Eve, the last chance to get anything.

There wasn't much left in the toy department. Of course, there were piles of jigsaws, educational games, encyclopedias, and children's writing paper – all the things that nobody ever wants. But Aggro had something else in mind: Action Man – a model soldier with a sub-machine gun. You worked him with a remote control, and you could make him move on wheels under his feet, fire the gun and light up his eyes all at the same time. Great! His best friend at school, Ben, had got one for his birthday. Chrissie hadn't decided what she wanted.

There was no sign of any Action Men. Dad went up to the counter and asked. "We're out of them," said the assistant. "We've got Action Kid, though – the same thing. Big pile there, in the corner." He led the way over.

Action Kid, as far as Dad could see, was exactly the same as Action Man. Large shiny box, with a pane of celluloid on the front. Soldier inside, with a plastic gun, batteries and a remote control. Aggro, however, was suspicious. It wouldn't do to turn up at school and find you'd bought some cheap imitation. The box looked wrong – it was crudely printed – and how did you know the Kid was going to do all the things that the Man did?

"Let's go to another shop, Dad," he said in his complaining voice. "I wanna get the real thing."

"You won't find any," said the assistant. "We sold our last three weeks ago. There's none to be had anywhere. These are a good line – same thing, not quite as expensive."

Aggro was examining the box. "The real ones are made in America," he said peevishly. "This one's useless." He pressed a sticky finger on the box. "Made in Bunyang." His face showed discontent.

Dad decided on some action himself. They'd have to meet Mum in an hour, and he wanted to do some shopping of his own. He put on his best car-salesman manner.

"Look, son. This one's good. Like the man says. You got the Kid, gun, control, batteries. Look what it does. Walks, fires, eyes light up in the dark. Then there's the packaging. Colour-printed box, inspection panel, easy to lift off lid." He winked at the assistant. "Bunyang? That's in America, ain't it? Somewhere in Florida. Part of Disneyland. Come on, mate, and wrap it up."

Aggro considered. There was clearly no choice to be had. It

might be all right. If it wasn't, well, he'd get money for Christmas and buy one afterwards. He wanted something now, anyway. "Okay," he said.

Chrissie had been looking round the shop. Nothing attracted her. She wondered if she could keep the money and spend it after Christmas. She walked up to the counter where Action Kid was being put into a bag and there, on the counter, she saw it: a set of Christmas Nativity figures, not very big, made of shiny glazed pottery, beautifully coloured. There was Joseph, Mary, a baby in a crib, three Wise Men, two shepherds and an angel. There was also a little, coloured dish with a candle in it, which you could light up and place by the group when it got dark. "Oh, lovely," she said, and started handling the figures.

"Cissy toys," said Aggro at once. Chrissie ignored him. "I'd like these, Dad, please."

"How much are they?" asked Dad. The man peered at them. "That's the last one left," he said. He mentioned a price.

"What are you taking off?" asked Dad, going back to being a salesman. "They're shop-soiled, aren't they? Been on display. Worth a discount. Dusty, look!" He polished off a bit of imaginary dirt from the third Wise Man.

"They'll go in the sale next week," said the assistant. "I tell you what, as you're buying the other toy, I'll do them for half price." Even Dad could find no fault with that. "We'll have them," he said.

The figures were carefully wrapped in tissue paper and put in a box. Chrissie produced her money. "I'll pay for the other one by credit card," said Dad, and flourished his piece of plastic. The man took it, made up a bill and gave it to Dad to sign, along with a pen. Aggro stood watching.

"Dad," he said, "why … ?"

Immediately, Dad, with surprising speed, said, "Shut up. Go somewhere else. Kids!" He made a face at the shopman. Chrissie, watching unobtrusively from the side, saw him write slowly and carefully, "T. Rycraft". The sale was completed, and two carrier bags were handed over. They walked out of the shop.

"Dad," started Aggro again. "Why hasn't your card got your name on it?"

Dad looked round quickly. "Ssssh!" he hissed. "Don't make trouble. Okay, it's someone else's card. Bloke at work. I did him a favour, and he lent me his card. All legal and above board. But don't tell people, see."

They came out of Sainsworth's, walked through the shopping centre, under an arch and into a courtyard. Something strange was happening. People were looking up into the air and pointing. A voice came from high up. "I'm going to jump!"

There was a row of shops, four storeys high, and a ledge going along the windows of the top storey. A man stood on the ledge, dressed in jeans and an old sweater. He was shouting.

"What's going on?" said Dad. One of the shopkeepers had come out. It was the manager of a takeaway shop selling burgers and chips. He looked furious. "Bloke up there gone round the bend. Saying he'll throw himself off. He'll hit the ground outside my shop. Good for trade, that'll be! They'll never get the marks off the pavement."

Dad considered. Nobody seemed to be doing anything. No police, nothing. "How d'you get up there?"

"Go up our stairs to the next window," said the manager. "I can't. I've got to look after my shop." He showed no sign of going back to his customers.

"Why don't you go up, Dad?" said Aggro suddenly. "Like you did in Special Operations? Get him down." Dad looked at him. He felt the challenge. "Okay," he said. "Show us the stairs. Chrissie, Aggro, you stay here."

Three minutes later, the spectators saw Dad open a window on the top storey and climb out on to the ledge. The upset man stopped shouting and looked round.

Dad decided humour was the best approach.

"Watch out, mate," he said. "You'll fall off if you aren't careful. Make an awful mess on the floor."

The upset man turned his eyes towards Dad. Curious eyes they were. Was he drunk, or drugged? "I'm finished," he said. "I'm going to finish it all."

"Pull yourself together," said Dad urgently. "Come down. Come on. I've got the window open here."

"You don't understand," said the man. "I've lost her. I'm all alone. All alone over Christmas. I can't stand it. D'you see? I can't stand it." He raised his voice to a shout.

Dad thought. You had to establish contact, somehow. Touch them, like. Give them a hand – human warmth. He put out his hand.

"Come on, mate," he said. "Catch hold my hand. I'll help you in through the window."

The upset man reached out and caught Dad's hand. He gripped it. Dad winced. The grip was terrific. The man began to babble. "I can't stand it. Got to end it. All alone. Everyone gone." He swayed on the ledge. Dad tried to pull his hand away. He was suddenly struck with terror. "If he goes, he'll pull me with him."

"Let go my hand, you fool!" he shouted. "Watch out below!

Get away!" Thoughts raced through his head. "Get the police. Ambulance. Fire. Quick!" There seemed to be no movement on the ground. It was like a film that had suddenly stopped. Everyone below was frozen still.

"Police!" wailed the upset man. "Not police. Not prison. I can't stand it. I'm going." The man's body swayed again. Dad, sweating, fought to free his hand. "Let go!" he hissed through clenched teeth. "Christ, save us."

"All right," said a quiet voice from the window behind him. Somebody took hold of his coat. "I've got you." The voice spoke to the upset man. "I'm a friend," it said. "Tell me what's wrong."

The upset man stopped swaying and turned towards the voice. "Who is it?" he said. "Is it the police?"

"No, not the police," said the voice. "I'm a friend. I've come to help you."

The upset man suddenly burst into tears. "I'm all on my own," he sobbed. "I've lost her. I'm all on my own, all over Christmas."

"Do you want me to help you find her?" said the voice.

The man gulped. "Yes," he said.

"I'll help you," said the voice. "Now, let go this man's hand. Let him go. I'm going to help you." Dad felt the grip relax, then the man dropped his hand. Dad wiped his face with his free hand. His face was wet.

"Ease yourself inside now," said the voice. Dad edged backwards, and got himself into the room. He stood up shaking. Gorblimey! It was that vicar, the one he'd been rude to half an hour ago.

"Come inside now," said the vicar to the upset man. "We'll go and find her. If you're on your own at Christmas, I know some people who'll look after you."

"I want that," said the upset man. "I really want that. Please help me." He shifted nearer to the window. The vicar put out his hand to guide him. "Come inside. Carefully now. Step backwards. Put your foot here. Good." The man reversed himself through the window, and stood in the room. There was a burst of cheering from below.

Feet sounded on the stairs, and two police officers came in. The upset man quailed. "It's all right," said the vicar. "They won't hurt you. I'm going to look after you." There was a further noise outside, and in ran Chrissie and Aggro.

"Well done, sir," said one of the officers to the vicar. "Saved us a tricky job there. Now then" – to the upset man – "what's all this about?"

The vicar spoke. "I'd like to help a bit. Our friend here wants a good talk about things. He's got to find someone he's lost, and he's worried about Christmas. I can take him away for a chat and I know a house where he'd be very welcome for Christmas." He conferred with the police officer.

Aggro and Chrissie came up to Dad, looking at him wonderingly. "Hey, Dad," said Aggro. "We saw you on the window sill!"

Dad took out a handkerchief, and mopped his forehead. He felt in need of a long, long, very long drink. Something else fell out of his pocket as well, and dropped on the floor. It was the credit card. The other policeman stooped and picked it up.

"Here you are Mr … Mr Rycraft," he said, reading the name as he handed it back. "I suppose you were a witness to all this. I don't think it's likely to go any further, but I'll take down your name and address to be on the safe side. Just tell me where you live, and I'll write it down." He took out his notebook.

"Fifty-eight Sandilands, Brierleigh," said Dad mechanically. The policeman, speaking aloud, started writing. "T Rycraft, number 58 … " Dad gave a start of horror. He tried to speak, but his voice came out with a croak. "That is, that's not my name … Not Rycraft. It's not my card. It belongs to a friend of mine and I'm using it for him."

"Using it, eh?" said the policeman, stopping his writing and looking at Dad. "Just what does that mean, sir?"

Dad gave a nervous laugh. "Well, I mean, not using it, of course. Looking after it. That's what I should have said. Looking after it for him. Friend of mine." His voice tailed away.

"I see, sir," said the policeman, as if he didn't. "Well, could you just tell me your proper name?"

"R J Smart," said Dad humbly. His cheeks were crimson red. The policeman wrote it down with the address and put away his notebook.

"All right, sir. You look a bit poorly. Bit of a shock for you. In our line, these things happen all the time – you get used to them." He turned to his colleague. "Everything okay, Mike?"

Apparently it was. The vicar was taking charge of the upset man. He turned to Dad. "Thanks for your help," he said. "It was good of you to get involved. You kept him talking. Sorry you got a fright. Go home and have a drink! Happy Christmas, anyway." He held out his hand and Dad shook it limply. The vicar, the upset man and the police began to leave the room. Dad and the kids filed after them.

When they reached the ground floor, a crowd had gathered round the door of the takeaway. The vicar was greeted by a round of applause. "Well done!" The manager offered him free burgers and chips whenever he liked to look in. Dad pushed his way through the crowd in the other direction, his cheeks burning. He needn't have worried. Nobody noticed him go.

They walked towards the car park. Aggro was chattering again. "Dad, was he really going to jump off? Why did he grab your hand? Why did you let that vicar take over?" Dad came out of his dream. His patience snapped. "Just shut up, and leave me alone," he said.

Mum was waiting by the car. "What's happened?" she said. Aggro burst out. "There was a man on a ledge. He said he was going to jump off! Dad went up to talk to him. Then he grabbed Dad's hand. Then there was this vicar. He took over and he got the man out." Mum listened. She had long ago learnt not to believe more than ten per cent of anything that Dad got involved in! It was all over, anyway, and no one was hurt. "We're late," she said. "Let's go home."

By the time they drove home to Brierleigh, Dad's spirits were beginning to rise again. Being in his car always made him feel good. He looked in the mirror to see if the police were about, put down his foot and got the car to go as fast as was possible in a queue of cars in a 30-mile speed limit. "Careful!" said Mum. He turned on the radio and filled the air with a blend of pop music and Christmas carols. He wound his window down and up again at the touch of a button. They turned off the main road and came down the lanes to the village. Two smaller cars nudged into the hedges to let them go by. Dad acknowledged them with a flick of the finger, as he surged magnificently past. He suddenly found his voice.

"I kept him talking," he said loudly, above the music. "He was going to jump. Then up came this other chap and we got him down together. Needed two of us. Police took my name. Said it might go further. I might get a police commendation – you know, bravery."

"Dad," said Aggro from the back seat, "why did you let that vicar take over?" The car veered a little, sped through the village, turned the corner into Sandilands, and drew up. They were home. Dad started unloading the drink from the back of the car – boxes of it. Mum went indoors with her bags. Aggro followed her.

"Mum," he said. "Was Dad really in Special Operations?"

"Special Deliveries, more like," said Mum, acidly. "He drove a truck – most of the time." For once, Aggro said nothing.

They had tea – burgers, chips and Christmas cake. Dad had two of his largest cans of lager. After tea, the kids opened their presents. Chrissie got out the Nativity figures and looked for somewhere to put them. There wasn't much space in the sitting room, with cards and trimmings and bottles all over the place. She thought of using the television, but Mum objected. "They'll get knocked off," she said.

Chrissie retreated upstairs to her bedroom. She cleared the small table which stood there and set out the figures on that. Joseph, Mary and baby Jesus. Three wise men on one side; two shepherds and the angel on the other. She put the candle in the middle. It looked beautiful. She lay on her bed to make sure she could see it from there. Later on she'd light it up and look at it in the dark.

Aggro was busy in the sitting room. With a bit of help from Dad, he put the batteries into Action Kid and into the remote control. He pressed the buttons, and the Kid sprang into life. He moved forward. His eyes glared and flashed. His sub-machine gun went of with a rattle. Aggro gave a yell of triumph. He made the Action Kid go round the table. Then he sent him behind the sofa. Then he mounted an all-out attack on the television. Hey, this was great. Better than Ben's. Just wait until he met him. They could have a combat with their men. Bet the ''id would win!

Bedtime came. Dad, who had been fortifying himself with lager all evening, put on his coat and announced he was going down to the pub for an hour with the lads. Mum went into the kitchen to do some jobs before her favourite television programme came on. Chrissie got Mum's reluctant permission to light the candle – "Only for ten minutes, mind, before you go to sleep" – and Aggro came upstairs with Action Kid. He wanted to try him out along the landing. Chrissie got ready for bed and lit the candle with a match. She climbed into bed and looked at the Nativity scene. It was beautiful and even better when she turned off her bedside lamp. The figures gleamed gently in the candlelight; their colours were more lovely than before. She switched on the lamp again and started reading her library book, looking back at the figures again and again.

There was a noise on the landing. Action Kid was coming. Aggro followed, holding the control. "Chrissie's got her cissy toys," he chanted. "I've got Action Kid. Attack! Attack! Ack-ack-ack-ack-ack!"

Action Kid advanced towards the table with its light and figures, his gun rattling loudly. Suddenly there was a silence. The Kid stopped dead in his tracks. Aggro pressed the control furiously. Nothing happened. He seized the Kid and shook him. He put him down and pressed the buttons again. Still there was no response. Chrissie, after a moment of alarm, looked on

serenely from her bed. Aggro became annoyed. He picked up
the Kid, took him on to the landing where the light was better
and examined him closely. How did Dad put in the battery? Ah,
he remembered. You took off the jacket, exposing the Kid's
plastic skin. On his back there was a catch, which you could
open. Inside, was the battery and a slit which led deeper into the
body. He held the control and pressed the button. Something
flashed inside the slit – there must be a loose wire. He put down
Action Kid, and tiptoed down the stairs in his pyjamas to get a
screwdriver from Dad's toolbox. Bother! That was in the
kitchen, and Mum was still in there. Hovering in the hall, he saw
something on the window sill by the coat rack: it was the plastic
card with T Rycraft's name on it. Dad had left it behind when he
went to the pub. Aggro picked it up, and brought it upstairs.

He poked the card into the slit and pressed the control.
Action Kid jerked into life. He took out the card and tried
again. Nothing happened. Could he fit in the card and close the
catch above it? That might get the Kid to work until tomorrow,
when Dad could put him right.

He had to press the card in very hard before he could close
the catch, but at last he managed it. He put back the Kid's jacket
and stood him up. "Advance! Attack!" He pressed the control
again, and the Kid started forward. The gun crackled with fury.
Aggro pushed open Chrissie's door and urged on the Kid again,
against the cissy toys on the little table. "Go in!" he shouted.
"Kill, kill, kill!"

Action Kid advanced towards the table, gave a tremendous
burst of firing and seemed to explode. Sparks shot out of the
gun and the Kid lurched forward, falling flat on his face in front
of baby Jesus. There was a smell of burning plastic. Aggro

rushed to the toy and slipped down the catch. Smoke wafted up and, from the inside of the Kid, he pulled out the credit card. It was scarred, twisted and useless. T Rycraft and the Action Kid had left this life together.

When Aggro had gone to his room, slamming the door, Chrissie remained reading for a while. Then she put away her book, turned out her bedside lamp and sat up for a few minutes, revelling in the Nativity figures, peaceful in the candlelight. She got up and blew out the flame. She laid down her head on the pillow and closed her eyes.

About an hour later she woke up. There was a clatter downstairs. The front door shut loudly and Dad's voice could be heard, singing noisily. Presently, there was the sound of talking in the sitting room – her mother's voice was raised. Clumping could be heard on the stairs, and the opening of a door. People were going to the bathroom. After a while, all went quiet.

She raised her head and looked at the Nativity scene. She could still see it in the streetlight which shone through the bedroom curtains. It glimmered, paler than before, as if in the moonlight. And then, far off, she heard another sound: mellow, distant, compelling. The church bells were ringing out as they had done for centuries, ringing out the news of Christmas. Something very old seemed to come from outside into the ordinary, modern house. She wondered what it was, but could not think. She burrowed into the pillow and went to sleep.

It was Christmas morning. Mum, with a dressing gown on, was in the sitting room. She drew the curtains apart, and picked up a wrapped present from under the Christmas tree. "What silly paper," she thought. She read the label, "From Sharon", and tore the parcel open. "Red blouse. Too small – I need a 14. Change it next week, in Sainsworth's." She looked at another, "Love from Dee". She opened just one end of this, and pulled out a pair of green tights. "Same as last year. She knows I never wear them."

She put down the presents and went upstairs, impatiently. On the landing she called out, "Rob! You still in the bathroom?"

Dad opened the bathroom door and came out, looking white. "I feel hung over," he said. "It wasn't the lager – it was the port on top. I've had some altar-shelters, I mean alka-seltzers."

"I'm waiting to do my hair," complained Mum. "You've been in there ever so long, and the kids were inside for hours."

Dad shuddered. Those kids. Up at dawn, they were, making a noise and breaking into his coma. At least it was quiet now. They must have gone outside.

They had. Aggro, in his new football strip, was kicking a ball on the grass beside the house. His friend, Steve-next-door, was skidding along on roller-skates, having a kick at the ball whenever it came his way.

Chrissie was on her new bike. She rode it up and down the road a couple of times, and then, as nothing else was happening, she thought she would go for a ride. "Round the world" it was called. You turned right, as if you were going out of the village, but if you followed the lane, you came back into the village on the south side. She quickened her speed and passed the boys in a flash. Behind her she heard Aggro shout, "Goal! What are you staring at, Steve?"

It was exhilarating to leave the village behind, and to feel the cold air on her face after the beery smell of the house. The bike was incredibly more powerful and easy to pedal than the old one. It was higher too – she seemed to fly along, like a bird, and she could see a long way over the roadside hedges. Everything was wet from the overnight rain, but the clouds were moving east, and gaps of blue were opening up between them. The last clouds coming over from the west were like great purple sacks, spilling out streams of white and cream. Shafts of sunshine were beginning to light up the skies.

There was not a soul on the roads. She coasted down a hill, and turned right towards the village. By the time she reached the turning to her house, it seemed too soon to go back. So she pedalled on through the village. Here too all was deserted. The houses, washed by the rain and delicately lighted by the pale winter sun, looked like houses in a painting – as if they had gone to sleep and would never wake up.

She turned her bike up the lane that led to the church. She thought she would have a look inside. There might be a Christmas tree and a crib, like there had been years ago when she went there with her school to sing carols. She got off her bike and leaned it against a wall, ready for a swift getaway if a vicar or someone came out. She looked at the notice board. "Christmas Family Service, 11 a.m.," it said. The church clock pointed to five past ten. There was no one about. She opened the churchyard gate, and walked inside.

She went into the porch, and looked at the door. It had a heavy, iron ring instead of a handle. She lifted it and tried to turn it. It resisted her attempt. Either it was locked, or the rust and damp of years was frustrating her wish to get in. She dropped the ring, and it hit the wood behind it with a sharp crack like a knocker on a door. She withdrew, disappointed, into the churchyard, and out into the lane. She got on her bike again.

If you went down the lane past the church, you soon came to the edge of the ridge on which the village was built. The lane plunged down a short, steep hill towards the river, where the ford used to be. At the top of the hill she stopped her bike and looked out westwards, over the river and the fields beyond. There was an amazing sight. The last raincloud was coming from the west, with a ghostly shower of rain underneath it. On this shower shone the rising sun, now free of clouds, producing a perfect rainbow, brilliant against the purple cloud behind it, its ends apparently close by in the fields. She was filled by a strange exaltation. Her surroundings seemed to drop away. The world felt newly made. It was not the humdrum world of Brierleigh, with the well-known roads that led to school and shops, but a new world calling her to come. Out there, beyond the rainbow, lay Cornwall, which she had never seen; the Atlantic; America; forests, mountains, people. She thought, "I could go there – on my own. Leave our house, and all the family rows." She vowed "I will, one day!"

She remained, standing on the lip of the ridge above the river, for several minutes, gazing to the west. The raincloud passed above, dropping its shower upon her. The rain fell cold against her face for a couple of seconds, and then stopped, almost before she had noticed it. She gave a shiver. She felt as if she was no longer looking at this beautiful new creation, but that she was part of it: like the sky, the cloud and the river. The rain, in touching her, had brought her in. Then she got a shock. With a sudden clatter of wings, a bird rose in the air, just in front of her. It was a large bird, its wings extended as it beat them to ascend, its colour purest white against the evergreens beside the churchyard. It flew up, over her head, towards the east. Her eyes followed it, and her body wrenched the bike round to face in the same direction. The bird, gleaming in the light, flew straight towards the sun, and disappeared into its dazzle.

A car drew up, and somebody got out. She became aware that people might be coming for the service. She pressed down her legs on the pedals, and moved off. She rode back through the village to her home, breathless with a strange excitement. Aggro was looking out of the front door. He had taken off his football strip, and had on his ordinary clothes. He gave a shout, "Hey, Chrissie. Come to church!"

He startled her. None of them ever went to church; they didn't even talk about it, least of all Aggro, and she could not imagine any reason why he should want to be going now. Anyway, their parents wouldn't let them. She got off her bike, put it against the wall and ran up the path. Aggro remained by the door. As she came towards him, he said it again. "Come on. I'm going to church."

"Why?" she said, breathing fast.

"Steve's going," said Aggro, as if there was no need of further explanation.

"Why is he?"

"His parents are. They've got his gran staying. I'm going."

"All right," she said. "I'll come."

Aggro immediately put his head inside the hall, and shouted, "Mum, we're going to church."

Mum looked out of the kitchen. She was holding a hairdrier. "What d'you mean? Church! We're going to auntie's at half past twelve."

"That's okay, Mum. It's a home fixture, and the kick-off's at eleven. It only lasts about half an hour," said Aggro, who seemed to have become an instant authority on local church services.

"Well, Chrissie can't go," said Mum firmly. "I need her to wrap things up."

"Steve wants her to come," said Aggro, equally firmly. "Mum, we'll do them when we get back."

Mum started out of the kitchen at this rebellion, but at that moment Dad emerged from the sitting room, blocking the way. Aggro switched his attention to his father. "Dad, we're going to church. Want to come?"

Dad made a face. "Catch me going! The last time I went in one, I came out with your Mum."

Aggro seized a coat and slammed the door. He and Chrissie pedalled down the road. After Mum had delivered some sharp remarks to Dad about the way he let the kids behave, Dad went back into the sitting room for refuge. "Church? Our kids?" he asked himself. He wondered if it was something to do with the alka-seltzer. He shook his head, reached for a glass and opened another can of lager.

The church was very full and they sat with Steve, but behind and therefore out of sight of his parents (plus his gran). The holly was green and red against the stone of the arches, and some carols were sung which they knew from school. There was one awkward moment when the collecting bag came round, because they had not brought along any money. But Aggro handed it on, with a lordly gesture, as if he had put in a whole handful of notes.

The Major, who was counting the collection in the vestry after the service, said, "Good lot of people. Some new faces. Never seen the Smart boy and girl in church before."

"One boy spent the whole time looking at the girl," said Miss

Vereker, who was hanging up the choir robes in a cupboard. "The girl just stared into space. I wonder why they came."

The vicar, who was also there, said nothing, but made a mental note to ask the three to the new club, when it started after Christmas.